A COLD

KILLING

AND OTHER STORIES
OF DEATH AND MURDER

Stories by
Mel Goldberg

Rolemi Publishers

Also by Mel Goldberg

Poetry: *The Cyclic Path* Rolemi Publishers, 1990
           Sedona Poems   Rolemi Publishers, 2001

Prose: *Choices*, (A Novel) iUniverse, 2003

A special thanks to my life partner Bev Kephart for her constant encouragement.

ISBN: 978-0-9827345-0-6

Cover and story illustrations by Bev Kephart

For my progeny:
Robin, Leslie, Mike,
Lauren, Jennifer, Rachel, Ricki,
Jeri and Avi,
(listed by age)

ACKNOWLEDGEMENTS

"Cyanide Suicide" first appeared online at *Orchard Press Mysteries*, Winter 2001

"The Broken Lamp" first appeared online at *Hand Held Mysteries*, Spring, 2002

"A Page Turner" and "A Penguin Classic" were first printed in *FMAM (Futures Mystery Anthology Magazine)* in Spring 2004 and August 2006 respectively.

"He who does not prevent a crime when he can, encourages it."

Seneca (Roman philosopher, First century CE)

TABLE OF CONTENTS

A COLD KILLING

Detective Aaron Guerevich and his fiancée Ann Berendt had come to spend the New Year's holiday in Chicago, the city where Guerevich had grown up. Instead of relaxing at their hotel or strolling along Michigan Avenue, they walked down the stairs to the basement of the Rogers Park police station on the Near-North side. Their shoes clanked on the metal stairs and echoed across the concrete floor. Like entering a cold, dimly lit hell, they walked along a corridor and stopped in front of a cell.

"Hello, Jaime." Guerevich spoke softly through the prison bars. He squinted, his brown eyes peering into the dim cell, lit by a single recessed light in the ceiling.

"Who are you?" Jaime remained seated on his bed, looking out from his abyss. His dark skin and his close-cut black hair a complement to his round Mestizo face, smooth and hairless, except for a bushy mustache, which drooped down past the corners of his mouth.

"I'm an old friend of your Uncle Roberto. This is my friend, Ann Berendt."

Ann smiled, wrinkling her eyes, showing white and even teeth. She involuntarily raised a hand to her hair to smooth errant strands of hair. "We're here to help you if we can. Aaron saw the article about the murder in the Chicago Tribune yesterday.

"Really?" Sarcasm gave an edge to Jaime's voice. "How did you know Tio Roberto?" Jaime stood up from his bed, a thin mattress on top of a hip-high cinderblock rectangle attached to the wall, and walked toward the two strangers standing outside the steel door.

"I met him a long time ago, when I was a teenager. Ann never had the pleasure but I remember your uncle as a very kind and honorable gentleman. It's a shame what happened."

Jaime looked down and shook his head. "Yes, it is." He looked up at Guerevich, his voice resolute. "I had nothing to do with his death."

He put his hands on the bars. Moisture glistened in his eyes. His large chest filled the top half of his orange jumpsuit but his feet disappeared in wide legs several inches too long. "I told the police that I was at my home when he was killed."

"Was anyone with you?"

"Yes, someone was with me. But I can't tell who without getting her in trouble. She and her husband are legally separated, but if anyone knew about us, it would put her in a very difficult position."

"I think I understand your dilemma," said Guerevich, taking out his small notepad and scribbling hastily. He looked up. "But you could be facing life in prison. Or worse. Surely, she'll come forward."

"She will if I ask her. But I won't do that to her. There must be another way to prove I am innocent."

"Have you told this to your lawyer?" asked Ann.

"That fucking idiot. Sorry. He said if I refused to tell him who she is, he would be unable to get her testimony, and he wouldn't handle the case. He said any other lawyer would do the

8

same. I didn't think a public defender could refuse to take a case. I'll probably get one who will no doubt tell me to plead some lesser charge."

"But you'd still go to jail for years," said Ann. "Will you at least talk to us?"

"Why should I talk to you? What can you do?"

Ann shook her head. "Maybe nothing. But we'd like to try."

Jaime looked at her. "At least you're being honest."

Guerevich asked one of the guards to carry a request to District Commander David Boggs that Jaime be allowed to meet with them in one of the conference areas. After a short wait, the three were taken through the large family meeting space to a small room with a long white folding table, scarred with cigarette burns and drink stains. Jaime shuffled, his leg chains clinking on the concrete floor. A chain around his waist attached to his wrists limited his arm movement. Once in the room, he clacked into a wooden chair and bent down to scratch his chin.

"Do you have any change?"

"Change?"

"Yes. You can get me a cup of coffee and a candy bar from the machine. The guard will free my left arm so I can eat and drink in the room."

Ann bought coffee for all of them and two candy bars for Jaime.

Once they were seated and the door was partially closed, Jaime Gutierrez asked his question again. "How did you know my uncle?"

Guerevich set his note pad on the table. " I first met him when he worked for my father. My father helped him get a job at a small factory."

"The one that manufactured nuts and bolts? So that man was your father."

"Yes. But my father knew he was too intelligent to spend his life running a machine. After a year on the job, your uncle discovered a way to modify the machines, and developed a process that allowed them to run faster without reducing the quality of the product."

Jaime nodded. "Tio Roberto told me about that. He didn't patent the process because he was an illegal. He didn't want to apply and expose himself."

"That's right. My father patented the process and leased it to the company, giving Roberto the income. When your uncle finally got his citizenship, my father sold him the patent for one dollar. After your uncle moved to Chicago, I saw him when he returned to Arizona for visits. He often stayed at our house."

"So why are you doing this? Helping me?" He sipped his coffee with his free left hand.

"It's the kind of thing my father would do. I believe it's necessary for every man to do what he can to help others. I need to understand whatever you can tell me about your uncle's death. Start at the beginning."

Ann reached in her large purse and took out a yellow legal pad. Then she looked at Jaime. "I'm ready."

"It's hard to believe any of this. I am being accused of the murder of my uncle, Roberto Gutierrez, because I am his only living relative. Tio Roberto always talked about your father, the man who helped him get started in this country, the friend who changed his life. Tio Roberto invested the money he made, and when he moved to Chicago, he purchased a small manufacturing company that also turned out nuts and bolts."

Ann scribbled the information on her pad. She looked up at Jaime. "How did you come to be raised by Roberto?"

"Seventeen years ago, my father, my mother, and my two sisters were killed while they were traveling in Mexico, on the narrow road from Guadalajara to Tepic. I didn't go with them because of summer school. That's when Tio Roberto took me in." Jaime paused and looked at Ann. "There is no way I would repay him by shooting him. Why should I? I had everything I ever wanted. He even helped me become a businessman. I own four McDonald's restaurants. Do you think I could have done that without his help?" Tears began to seep from Jaime's eyes and run down his face, getting lost in his bushy mustache. He instinctively reached up with his right hand to wipe them away, but the chain prevented his hand from reaching his face. "Damn." He threw his hand into his lap as the chain banged against the arm rest of the chair.

Ann handed him a tissue and he wiped his face with his left hand.

"Where was he killed?"

"In his home. He has a large house overlooking the lake on North Sheridan Road, just south of Evanston."

"We need the address in case we want to see it," said Ann.

"5703 North Sheridan."

"Exactly when did it happen?" She continued to write.

"The night of December 12. The news reported it was one of the coldest nights of the month. The temperature dropped to ten below. That's one reason I stayed at home."

"Any witnesses to the shooting?"

"There is a neighbor, Charles Andreesen. He told the police he heard three shots and rushed to the house. He claimed he recognized me, and saw me run out through the back door."

"We need to talk to this Andreesen." Ann added the note to her list of things to do.

"I hope you get more from him than the police did. I don't know why he said he saw me. I wasn't there that night. But I was arrested. No bail. The DA said she considered me a flight risk. Even though I have roots in the community, I have family in Morelia. My stupid lawyer didn't even fight her request for remand."

Guerevich grimaced. He had run into overworked assistant DAs before, rushing to get to their next case. "Is there anything else you can tell me? How about the name of the woman you were with?"

"I can't tell you her name. But my uncle always kept a large amount of cash in his house. It was kind of a joke, but he kept it in the freezer. He often laughed about his cold cash."

"How much did he keep?" asked Ann, writing the information in her notebook.

"Sometimes as much as $200,000. He stored it in a large box labeled *Queso de Oaxaca*. When the police searched the house after the murder, there was no box and no cash in the freezer. Or anywhere else in the house. I told the police but they didn't believe me."

"Well, we'll see what we can do." Guerevich wanted to reach out and hug the young man, or at least shake his hand, burt he knew police regulations forbade any physical contact between visitors and inmates. When they left the Rogers Park station, it was almost noon.

Ann grabbed Guerevich by the arm when they reached the landing at the top of the stairs. "What the hell do you think you'll be able to do?" she half whispered. "We're not in Scottsdale. We're in Chicago on vacation. I thought we could give him some moral support, and now I feel as if I'm back at work."

"You know I can't walk away. I have a chance here to do a mitzvah."

Part of the reason Guerevich became a cop was his Jewish religious belief which required him, both as a human being and a member of his religious community, to help others. He believed that performing a mitzvah, literally a commandment from God, often translated as a good deed, helped him come closer to achieving holiness.

He smiled at Ann, put his arm around her shoulder, and squeezed her to him. She put her arms around his waist and hugged him. "I know. It's one of the reasons I love you."

After a quick kiss, they walked outside into the cold afternoon. Guerevich put on his gloves and smiled at Ann. "Come on. I'm hungry. That coffee and bagel at the hotel this morning is long used up."

He remembered a deli in Rogers Park, they discovered it had closed years before.

"Well, now I know how we're going to spend our New Year's holidays, I wish it would snow. I've never really been in snow."

"Never? Never went skiing when you lived in Tahoe?"

"Never spent a winter there."

They waved down a taxi, who took them to Ada's, a new north side deli.

They sat and ordered. Guerevich sipped his coffee and looked around at the large restaurant, unlike the Ada's in the

Northbrook suburb he remembered from twenty years earlier. After a few minutes, their food arrived.

Ann spread spicy mustard on her pastrami sandwich. "I suppose Jaime doesn't have access to his uncle's estate."

Guerevich took a bite of his cheese omelet, put his fork down and sipped his coffee again. "He must have some money of his own. Maybe he owns stock in Roberto's company."

"I don't understand why this Andreesen fellow would lie about seeing him? If it is a lie."

"That's something we'll have to find out from him. Do you have any contacts in forensics here in Chicago?"

"You may be in luck. An old boy friend got a job here in Chicago after he left Tahoe. I haven't really kept in touch with him, but if he's still there, I'm sure I can turn on the charm and get him to do a few favors for me -- I mean us."

"Very funny. Just don't turn on too much charm."

"Well, I heard from a mutual friend he had a wife and two kids and he'd gained about thirty pounds. And he was pudgy when I dated him. Believe me, you have nothing to worry about."

After lunch, they took a bus to downtown Chicago to see the lights along State Street and look at window displays. From his childhood, Guerevich remembered the mechanized displays at Marshall Fields and Sears. He recalled the crowds that stood outside watching articulated elves and Santas moving their arms mechanically and laughing as they seemed to work at their benches while trains whizzed around miniature towns and train stations.

As dusk arrived, snow started to fall, large flakes whirling and spinning in the glow of street lights, landing gently on hats and coats, giving a red-cheeked Currier and Ives look to shoppers along Michigan Avenue.

When Guerevich suggested they walk back to The Drake Hotel, Ann complained that her nose and ears might freeze and fall off. They taxied back, had dinner, and spent an evening planning their strategy for the next day. Ann was to contact her ex-boyfriend, and Guerevich hoped to get permission from the Chicago police to talk to Andreesen.

Police movies and television shows try to add drama by portraying jealous disputes, detectives in one bureau getting angry when those in another department take over, as though they all worked on commission. The truth is overworked police departments usually welcome legitimate assistance from any source.

David Boggs, Commander of the Rogers Park Twenty-fourth District, gave Guerevich permission to question Andreesen. "Normally, I wouldn't do this, but you're an ex-Chicago cop and you had a good rep here. Besides, he may just tell you something that he wouldn't say to one of our guys. Just don't do anything to mess us up."

"Don't worry. I'll treat this one as if it were my own."

Ann got an escort to visit the crime lab. Guerevich took the Devon bus to Sheridan Road and walked the few blocks to Andreesen's. The temperature had fallen to the low 20s and the sun was a small cold fire in the sky.

Within seconds after Guerevich rang the bell, Andreeson, wearing a sweater and wrinkled chinos, opened the door. Several inches shorter than Guerevich, he had a halo of white hair around his head and his stomach protruded over his belt.

"Mr. Andreesen? I'm Aaron Guerevich from Phoenix. I'm doing a follow-up investigation on the death of Roberto Gutierrez. May I come in?"

"Well, I tell the Chicago cops everything ten times already. I don't want to tell story again." Andreeson spoke with a strong Norwegian accent.

"It's been a long time since I lived in freezing weather, and I'm not used to it."

"I guess it don't matter. Come in. One more time don't make no real difference."

Andreesen invited Guerevich in and made coffee. Walking back into the living room, he said, "Dis weather too cold for you? I hear blood thins out in hot climate like Phoenix. Where I come from, blood run very thick." He looked at Guerevich and smiled.

"I grew up in Chicago, but I guess I've become a warm weather person." He waited until Andreesen sat in the large chair and sipped his coffee before asking his first question.

"I don't want to take up too much of your time. Exactly where you when you heard the shots?"

14

"Actually, I was outside the house." Andreesen set the cup in the saucer he held in his hand. "I go to my garage to get my second pair of glasses from my car. Earpiece of my good pair lost a screw, and I have to hold them on my face. As I left garage -- my garage, it's not attached to house -- I hear the shots. Three. I rush over to house of Mr. Gutierrez, and find front door open. I run inside and see his nephew. I see him clearly like I see you. He look at me. Then he turn and run out through back door. That damn kid got everything handed to him on silver plate, and he do this. Ach, kids today."

"You say 'kid'? He's 32 or 33. Did you see him often?"

"Well, I see him for years. Always hanging around, wanting more. The old man buy him four McDonalds, but that ain't enough. He want two more. Said he couldn't make decent money unless he own five or six."

Guerevich wrote in his note pad. "I understand. Then what happened?"

"When I run in, I see Mr. Gutierrez on the floor and call 9-1-1, but of course, it was too late, even though it only took them couple minutes to get there."

"You say you were outside? You had retrieved your glasses from your car?"

"Yah. That's right."

"So you had your glasses on when you ran to the house?"

"Yes. Without glasses, I don't see much of anything other than what's in front of my face."

"You're sure it was Jaime. No doubt."

"Soon as I go into house, I see him. And he see me."

"Was he still holding the gun?"

"Don't remember seeing no gun. Young people today don't want to work hard. Don't want to take no responsibility."

"Do you know anything about the money Mr. Gutierrez kept in his house?"

"Why would he do that? Was there a lot?"

"I'm not aware of the exact amount. Jaime said his uncle kept money in the freezer."

"Don't know nothing about no money in freezer."

"Well, that's all I have to ask. I'm sure the police have the full report. Thanks for your time."

"No problem. It's a shame, though. Mr. Gutierrez was good man. He work hard for what he had. Not like nephew of his. Greed does strange things to people."

"Yes, it certainly does." Guerevich noted the new sofa and chair and he could smell the adhesive from new carpet, thick enough to show footprints.

Guerevich took the Outer Drive/Sheridan Road Bus back to the hotel. As it passed Foster Avenue, he involuntarily looked out over the lake, remembering the huge white Edgewater Beach Hotel that years before stood where the outer drive originally ended.

At the hotel, he found a message from Ann. She had information, and wanted him to meet her at the Artists' Cafe on Michigan Avenue, across from the Art Institute.

A five minute taxi ride brought him to the cafe. He crossed the wide sidewalk and tried to see Ann through the window, but the steamed glass kept him from looking in. He opened the door and saw her sitting at a table, a notebook open in front of her.

She looked up as he approached and took off his coat. "Hello, sweetie. Want some coffee?"

"As long as it's hot. My teeth are chattering. I know why my parents moved to Phoenix. I don't understand how they lived like this - it takes ten minutes to bundle up before you go outside, and then you can hardly move for all the clothes."

"Don't be a big baby. You don't hear me complaining, do you?"

"Well, I've read that women have an extra layer of fat to protect them. It's genetic." He smiled.

"Then maybe I'll just stay here with my genetic fat and you can go back to Phoenix by yourself. Stanley looked good. He joined an exercise club and lost almost fifty pounds."

"Stanley, huh. Very amusing. What'd you find out?"

"He was very helpful. He just didn't want his wife to know I had been here. I guess our relationship slipped his mind when he met her and he didn't bore her with details about us."

"Thanks. That's more information than I needed. What did you find out?"

"We did some research on Jaime. The man's clean. He has his own money. Small investments in Roberto's nut and bolt company and income from his four McDonalds. He's not rich, but he's not hurting for money."

"So he didn't have a motive. Except, he'd stand to inherit the house and his uncle's share of the business, which could be worth several million dollars."

"But he said he had a good relationship with his uncle. The old man was helping him financially. Gave him the seed money for the McDonalds' franchises and there are no records to indicate Jaime ever paid him back."

"That's the kind of man I remember Roberto to be. Did you find out anything about Andreesen?"

"There we have a different story. Until recently, Andreesen had money problems, according to Trans-Union Credit Reporting Agency. Four months behind on his house payment, a collection agency after him for back payments on his car, and maxed credit cards. You think he was desperate enough to kill Roberto?"

"I don't know. He struck me as the kind of man who might take advantage of a situation, but not a killer."

"Maybe there was a break-in, and the killer fled just as he said. And he helped himself to the money. I found out that recently, Andreesen made several cash deposits to his checking account, but none large enough to raise red flags at the bank. Suddenly he had enough money to pay his bills."

"He had new furniture and carpeting. He could have found the money before he called 9-1-1. If he waited ten or fifteen minutes, he could have searched the house before he called."

Ann sipped her latte. "He says he called immediately."

"The call came in to 9-1-1 at 8:46. That means the shots had to occur just after 8:45 to give Andreesen time to hear them, rush into the house, and see Jaime or whoever was there. Too bad no one else heard the shots."

Ann Smiled. "I have to save you again. I did some checking, because I had been thinking along the same lines. You know, two great minds and all that."

"That's why I love you. That's why we're meant to be together."

"Sure, sure. Anyway, there's a Sheridan bus that goes by the house about 8:35 if it's on time. I had Stanley contact the Chicago Transit Authority. Fortunately, the driver was on shift today, and I was able to speak to him. It turns out that because of light passenger traffic, he was running five minutes early. He heard the shots at 8:30. Stanley said that cold weather condenses sound and it travels faster."

"Why didn't the driver report it?"

"He said he thought they were backfires. He did say that three in a row is very unusual. Usually just one or two. He read about the murder in the newspaper, but when the police made an arrest, he didn't pay any more attention."

"So Andreesen had time - almost fifteen minutes - to search the place, take the money, and stash it somewhere."

"Why would he blame Jaime?"

"Didn't like him. He thought Jaime was a lazy kid, and just wanted his uncle to support him. He really doesn't understand the closeness of family ties in Mexican tradition. He said it himself when I talked to him. 'Greed does strange things to people.' But the timing and deposits aren't enough. We need something else."

"But what? Remember, we're just visitors. We really can't go barging around, uprooting a case that Chicago PD thinks is pretty well closed."

"I know. Well, let's head back to the hotel and sleep on it. Maybe something'll come to us."

In the hotel room, Guerevich turned the thermostat down to 65 degrees and they went to bed. Just before dawn, he woke up, intending to watch the sun rise over what he always thought of as his city. He wiped the fogged pane with a tissue. As he was about to throw it in the trash, his jaw dropped and he stared at the wet lump of paper in his hand. "How could I be so stupid." He ran back to the bed and shook Ann's shoulder. "Ann, wake up. The answer to the problem is here in front of us."

Ann squinted in his direction and rolled to one elbow. "What do you mean?"

"Come here."

She got out of bed and walked toward him.

He smiled at her nude body moving in slow motion from sleep. He took her hand and led her to the window. "Look out at the city. What do you see? Nothing, because the windows are steamed up. That's because it's warm inside and cold outside."

"So?"

"So, if Andreesen ran into the warm house from a sub-zero night, the first thing that would happen is his glasses would fog up. He admitted he's almost blind without them. There's no way he could have recognized Jaime or anyone else in that house. I don't think he killed Roberto. That's going to be up to the Chicago PD . But one thing seems certain. He did take the money. We need to talk with Captain Boggs."

Two days later, a search of Andreeson's house turned up fifty thousand dollars in cash in a box marked *Queso de Oaxaca*. He was arrested and Jaime was released.

Aaron and Ann took a taxi to The Hancock Center in Chicago's Commercial District. They looked at the skyscraper's distinctive X-bracing exterior, the structure's skin that is part of the spine that helps the building stand upright during high wind and has made the center an architectural icon.

They rode the elevator to the ninety-fifth floor to dine at *The Signature Room* and look out over Chicago and Lake Michigan. After dinner they drank champagne, danced, and held hands as they silently celebrated the New Year and watched the lights twinkle like diamonds over the city.

THE BROKEN LAMP

Donald Sackman skulked down the dark street, the only illumination a street light at the corner almost a block away. He kept a steel pry bar close to his leg as he trudged along. Turning into the yard of an old stucco house, he walked the 20 feet toward the door and climbed the three steps to the wooden porch that spanned the front of the house. The boards, warped and cupped with age and weather, made him remember his empty promise to sand and refinish them. He wore leather driving gloves, although it was November and the nighttime temperature in Scottsdale hovered at a mild sixty-seven degrees,. Propping the steel pry bar against the wall next to the door, he looked around before knocking. It took a few minutes for the curtained windows to brighten. The outside porch light had no bulb. He had removed it two days before.

"Who is it?"

"Me, Gramps."

"Donny?" The door opened slightly. The old man, hunched with age, looked up at his grandson's face. "What's wrong? It's three in the morning."

"I need to talk to you."

"Well, c'mon in. I'll make some coffee. I can't sleep anyway. What're you wearing gloves for. It's not that cold."

Donald hesitated in the doorway as Morton Sackman shuffled back through the living room, bracing himself as he walked past the oak table. The wiring in the old house allowed for no ceiling light, so the single floor lamp was the only illumination.

Donald reached back and picked up the pry bar before he entered the house. Stepping into the living room, he closed the door behind him.

Although he was right handed, Donald intentionally swung the bar with his left hand, striking his 85-year-old grandfather on the left side of the head, just above and behind his ear, believing that such a blow would cause instant death.

Blood splattered on his gloves and on the overstuffed chair. The old man flew sideways, his shoulder banging into the table. His body rebounded, knocking down and smashing the floor lamp. Taking a small flashlight from his pocket, Donald saw his grandfather's body sprawled across the center of the room, face down. In its narrow beam, he winced at the blood pulsing from the crushed skull onto the carpet. Blood and small clots of hair coated the pry bar in his hand. He knew without looking that blood had spattered his shirt, trousers, and jacket as well.

Donald stood quietly and listened. Silence, both inside and outside the quiet street of the old neighborhood.

"What if he's not dead," he thought.

As if he feared the old man would rise and admonish him, he raised the pry bar and smashed it into the back of the old man's head. He avoided the blood pooling before the carpet absorbed it, stepped over the small crumpled body and tiptoed to the floor safe in the corner. Kicking aside the throw rug that covered it, he worked the combination, removed the $250,000 he knew was there, and stood up, looking back at his dead grandfather.

"I wish it had been different, Gramps. Shit, I'm forty-two. How many more years did you expect me to wait?" Donald opened the door and turned the knob pin to the locked position. He went outside, closed the door, and using the clean end of the pry bar, he forced it into the jamb until it splintered and the door popped open.

He closed the door again, stood outside for a moment and listened. In the distance, he heard a siren, but scanning the street, he saw no house lights. He heard no doors opening. Fearful someone might see him, a dark figure hurrying down the street at three in the morning, carrying a bloody pry bar. As he turned the corner and continued up the block to his car, his shadow from the corner street light caught up with him and passed him. The rough cuticle on his thumb caught in the lining as he removed the right glove with his left hand and opened his car door. Once seated behind the wheel, he placed the glove and the pry bar in a plastic-lined cardboard box on the passenger seat. Using corn tongs he had placed on the floor of his car, he removed the left glove and put it in the box.

He drove home, showered, and put his blood-spattered clothes and shoes in a plastic bag. The next morning, he took the bag along with a load of scrap wood to the crusher at the landfill before he went to his office at Sackman Enterprises. His door was next to the office of Edelberto Gonzalez

Like Morton Sackman, Edelberto had known poverty as a young man, having been born in the tiny Mexican village of Bahuichivo in Chihuahua. They met when Morton had stayed in the village on a visit to Copper Canyon. Morton had been impressed with the younger man's attempt to establish a school in his village to teach young Mexican and Tarahumara men the trade of furniture-making. With financial backing from Morton, Edelberto's school became a reality. He then expanded and began a small import company to bring the handmade furniture to the United States.

Once his school and business were successful, Edelberto moved to Arizona and bought a four-bedroom house in Scottsdale. Being unmarried allowed him to travel regularly between the United States to Mexico.

Later that morning, Donald Sackman received a call from Edelberto Gonzalez.

"I'm a little worried, Donald. Your grandfather, he don't show up at the restaurant for the financial meeting this morning. And he don't answer his phone."

"Nothing to worry about, Ed," said Donald. "The other day, Gramps told me he was afraid he was coming down with a cold. He probably took some medicine and he's sleeping in. My guess is he doesn't want to be in a crowd for a few days. At his age, if a cold weakens his resistance, he could get something much worse."

"You probably right. I only wish he call me."

"You know how he is. He doesn't want people to worry about him."

"Your *abuelo*, he is good man. I have some papers from the business that he must sign. I can't take it over to him until *mañana* or the day after."

"Why don't I just come by your house later and pick them up. I'm going to see Gramps this evening. He promised to come over for dinner and watch a movie with me."

When Donald went to Edelberto's house, he carried with him a small box with gloves, a blood-spattered pry bar, and a plastic bag containing over two hundred thousand dollars. He entered the garage, which was always open, placed the box on a shelf behind a stack of papers, and knocked at the kitchen door.

Taking the papers from Edelberto, Donald promised to deliver them to his grandfather. "I'll see that they're signed and bring them to the office tomorrow."

At seven-thirty that evening, Donald Sackman, wearing faded jeans and a polo shirt, went to his grandfather's house. Standing outside the door, he called the police on his cell phone.

"My grandfather didn't show up for dinner, and when I phoned, there was no answer. I'm at his house now. It looks like the door's been forced open."

"What's the address? We'll have someone come by in a few minutes. Don't go in and don't touch anything."

In less than fifteen minutes, officers Ray Ziemansko and Philip Jameson met Donald outside the old stucco house. Ziemansko was a ten year veteran on the force, but Jameson was a young rookie. They both agreed the front door had been pried open. The curtains were drawn, and the house was dark.

Officer Ziemansko pushed open the door, but he could see nothing in the darkened room. Donald reached in and flipped the switch for the outside light, although he knew nothing would happen.

Ziemansko looked up at the fixture. "There's no bulb."

"There's a light switch on the other side of the room for the light in the dining area," said Donald. He walked through the room and turned on the light. There, sprawled across the middle of the living room floor, lay the body of Morton Sackman, the side of his head bashed in, and the back of his skull crushed. Next to his head was a puddle of nearly dried blood. Donald gasped and immediately moved toward his grandfather, but he was stopped by young Jameson. Ziemansko crouched next to the body and put his two fingers to the old man's throat.

"No pulse, and the body's cold."

"Don't touch anything," said Jameson, as he radioed the call to report a homicide, which brought a nod from Ziemansko.

Looking around, both officers observed the throw rug pushed against the wall in the corner. They told Donald to wait outside while they examined the room. Near the crumpled rug, they noted the door to the floor safe open. Ziemansko wrote his description of the scene as Jameson commented.

Within half an hour, Detective Aaron Guerevich was at the scene, his neat blue suit, white shirt and tie a contrast to his Chicago Cubs baseball cap. He asked Ziemansko what happened as he surveyed the room and did a preliminary examination of the body. Standing, he took out his note pad and began writing.

At five feet ten inches tall, Ziemansko looked up at the taller Guerevich. "I'll have to write up my own incident report," Ziemansko said. "When we got here, we saw the door had apparently been jimmied open. You can see the jamb's splintered."

"Right," Jameson said. "The house was dark when we got here, and Mr. Sackman, Donald that is, tried to turn on the outside light, but the bulb was missing. He walked through to the dining area and switched on the light there. That's when we saw the lamp had been knocked down and the body of his grandfather, the older Mr. Sackman, on the floor in the living room where you see him."

"No one moved the body?"

"No, sir. We didn't touch anything. Everything is exactly the way it was when we arrived."

Three hours after Donald Sackman had called the police, a little before midnight, the police photographer and the medical examiner's team walked into the house. They arrived at the same time as Guerevich's fiancée, forensic specialist Ann Berendt, and two other people from her lab. As they dusted for prints and outlined the body on the carpeted floor with yellow tape, the photographer took pictures. Using his liver thermometer, the medical officer determined that death had occurred about twenty hours earlier, between three and four AM the day before.

Before Guerevich walked outside to speak to Donald Sackman, he walked over to where Ann was dusting for prints.

"Anything usable?"

"Lot of prints here. But whose they are is anyone's guess. I'll run them through CODIS, and hope the killer has a record."

"I never understand something like this. This is one of the most brutal killings I've come across in a long time. Who'd want to kill an old man for a few dollars."

"It might have been a lot more than a few dollars, Aaron. All we found was a large folder with the deed to the house, an insurance policy for $100,000 with Donald Sackman as beneficiary, and a sealed envelope marked WILL with the name of an attorney. I'll take everything back to the lab, but there wasn't any money there."

"None?"

"Not even bank wrappers. To make matters worse, the M.E. thinks the killer delivered the blow to the back of the head post-mortem. The old man was probably dead before his body hit the floor. You coming by for breakfast?"

"Depends how long it takes at the station. I'll call if I can't make it." He pursed his lips in a kissing gesture before he walked outside to where Donald Sackman waited.

Guerevich indicated he had no more questions for the two policemen, but he wanted a copy of their report faxed to him as quickly as they completed it. He stepped outside and spoke to Donald Sackman, who reaffirmed what the policemen had said. He had expected his grandfather for dinner. When the old man didn't show and didn't answer his phone, Donald had driven to the house, observed the jimmied door, and called the police.

Guerevich took Donald Sackman back to the station and escorted him to one of the interrogation rooms.

"I'm not under suspicion, am I?" Donald said as he walked into the room.

"Of course not. Here we can have some coffee and talk. We just need to get as much information as we can. Anything you might tell us could be helpful., even if you might not think so."

Donald took a deep breath, sat on one of the metal folding chairs, and clasped his hands together on the table. Guerevich stepped out of the room and returned with two styrofoam cups filled with steaming coffee. He sat across from Donald.

"Did your grandfather make a habit of keeping money or other valuables in his floor safe?

"He once told me he kept enough in his safe to buy his house two or three times over. He might have had as much as three hundred thousand."

"That's quite a bit of money. Didn't he trust banks?"

"As a matter of fact, he didn't. His parents moved here from Chicago about 1930, when he was nine. He distrusted banks after they lost their home and all of their savings in 1929."

"How did he live? Did he have any income? Any investments?"

"Let me tell you a little about my grandfather. He must have told me this story a hundred times. As a young man, he picked cotton down near Casa Grande. He lived frugally and saved enough money to buy a small piece of property, which he sold for a profit. That's how he made his money, buying and selling property."

"He was still investing in property?"

"Actually, no. About twenty years ago, he started investing directly in small start-up companies. That's when I started to work for him."

"So he invested in these companies?

"Only ones he felt had potential. His only requirement was that he have a hand in running them initially. After the company was on its feet, he sold his portion to the original owners for a decent profit on his investment. He referred to these investments as projects."

"Did he have any, uh, projects recently?"

"His latest project was Edelberto Gonzalez, who formed a company to import handmade furniture from Mexico. Gonzalez started a school to teach young Mexican and Tarahumara men traditional Mexican furniture making. The school also taught them to read and write as well as giving them a trade."

"Gonzalez imported the furniture to sell here in Phoenix?"

"Yes. Unfortunately, the business wasn't doing well. In fact, it was losing money."

"You know quite a bit about his business. Accounting? Management?"

"A little of everything. Mostly, I was his go-fer. When he needed something, anything, he called me to get it, from coffee to sales reports."

"Did you like your job?"

"Yeah, sure. I mean, he was my grandfather. He always said he wanted me to take over after he, well, you know."

"Died?"

"Yeah."

"What about your parents?"

"They were killed along with my grandmother in a four-seater plane crash when I was ten. That's when I came to live with him. I studied accounting for two years at Pima College and then went to work for him."

Guerevich nodded and handed Donald a business card. "Well, thanks, Mr. Sackman. You've been very helpful. If you can think of anything else, please call me. I'll have one of our officers take you back to your car. And we'll keep you informed about our investigation."

"We won't need an autopsy, will we?" asked Donald, rising from his seat, his coffee untouched. "I mean, the cause of death is pretty obvious."

"I understand your concern. But the law requires an autopsy in homicide cases. You seem to be taking this very well. Were you close with your grandfather?" Guerevich rose and opened the door for Donald.

"Very close. But he was eighty-five. I knew his death was imminent, so I mentally prepared for it."

"Even so, this must have been unexpected." Guerevich stood in the doorway, half a head taller than Donald, who looked down and nodded.

"Totally."

Guerevich stepped aside to let Donald pass. "One last question. Did you have the combination to the safe?"

"No, I didn't. Gramps was very secretive about his money. He told me a copy of the combination was in his will. I guess the only other person who knew it was his lawyer. And probably his business partner, Edelberto Gonzalez."

When Donald left, Guerevich looked at his watch. Only eight AM. Still time for breakfast with Ann. He dialed her lab number, got her answering machine, and then called her at home. Her caller ID registered his name.

"Aaron, what's up. It's only eight in the morning. Don't even ask about Sackman. I dropped everything off at the lab and came home to sleep."

"Just wondered if you want to get some breakfast?" He paused waiting for her response.

"Did you go in to question Sackman this morning? Don't tell me. I know. Best to do it when everything's fresh. Why don't you come over here. I'll make some coffee. I think there's a bagel in the freezer."

Ann's apartment was a third floor walkup in a 1920 era brick building. The living room sported a wood floor with a fake fireplace, but the cooking area between the stove and the sink in the kitchen allowed for only one person. The original dining nook had been removed to make room for a small eating area. The large living room windows made the eating space cheerful, and her wrought-iron, glass topped kitchen table with old ice-cream parlor chairs, gave the room an open-air cafe flair.

An hour after his phone call, Guerevich sat at her small round table, put the last bite of cream-cheese-covered bagel into his mouth, and washed it down with a sip of coffee. "Nothing I like better than commercially made, frozen bagels. They have that unmistakable rubbery quality."

"No one said you had to eat it. You're certainly capable of making your own breakfast." She paused and glared at him. "In your own apartment."

"And miss out on your smiling morning face? Not a chance."

Ann sneered at him as she got up to pour herself another cup of coffee, her slippers plop-plopping as she walked. "I won't be in the lab until about ten today. I'm not expected to do the twenty-four hour shifts you guys pull."

"Okay, but when you get in, I want you to research Morton Sackman. Something odd about an old guy who keeps all his money in a floor safe and gives cash to indigent entrepreneurs."

"Speaking of old guys, have you talked to your father recently? He still doesn't understand why a Yeshiva boy would want to become a cop."

"Well, Chicago is a long way from here in both time and space. Besides, I spoke to him a few days ago. I think he's given up trying to get me to change my career. It's been almost eight years. Now about that research."

"Give me a couple of days. I do have other responsibilities in my job."

"I need it today. See what you can do." He smiled. "I'll stop in at the lab this afternoon."

"Please don't. You always expect me to drop everything and chat with you when I've got too much work to do.

That afternoon, disregarding Ann's warning, Guerevich walked down the stairs to Ann's lab to find out if she had been able to get any information on Morton Sackman.

"Well," she grumbled, shaking her head. "Considering you gave me a whole morning, I discovered what his grandson said is pretty much right on. The old man was a bit of an oddball when it came to money. He distrusted banks and had lots of money in his house."

"I need to know what Donald didn't tell me."

"According to public records, in the last two years Morton Sackman pumped almost $200,000 into a furniture import business called Gonzalez, Incorporated. The company did well for a while, but started losing money about eight months ago, and is now on the verge of bankruptcy. Slow sales, a weak economy, and rising costs. Maybe even frequent delays caused by searches from Mexican border guards. I've heard that sometimes trucks have to be completely unloaded and then reloaded."

Guerevich sat on a stool next to her work station. "That adds an interesting dimension to the murder. It's possible Edelberto wanted more money, and old Sackman was ready to throw in the towel. Donald said the old man only gave money to companies he believed had a future."

"But from what Donald told you, my guess is that Sackman wanted the business to succeed. But you're right. Gonzalez did have motive."

"That's the part I don't understand. If Sackman died, that effectively cut off his money."

"Edelberto Gonzalez had personally mortgaged everything he owned, and the assets of the business were only a fraction of what he owed."

"It's time to get a search warrant for Gonzalez's house. His financial difficulties make him a prime suspect. People have killed their own fathers for less."

In a search of Gonzalez's home, police discovered the plastic-lined cardboard box hidden on a shelf in the garage. The box contained a pair of blood-spattered gloves, a pry bar with blood stains and bits of hair, and $200,000 in cash in large zip-lock bags. Gonzalez was left handed. Since Morton Sackman had been struck from behind on the left side of his head, Gonzalez was immediately arrested on suspicion of murder.

He protested his innocence as he was handcuffed and led away from his house. "You got the wrong man. I loved that old man like he was my own father. I owe him everything. Why would I kill him?"

Because of the heinousness of the crime and Gonzanez's ties to Mexico, the judge confiscated his passport and denied bail, ordering Gonzalez held in jail pending his trial. The evidence, though circumstantial, was strong. Although he continued to protest his innocence at his arraignment, he had no alibi. The morning Morton Sackman had been murdered, Edelberto Gonzalez claimed to have been home alone, asleep in his bed. The Public Defender assigned to the case advised his client to plead guilty to second degree murder.

Three weeks following the homicide, after an expedited probate, Morton Sackman's will was disclosed. Guerevich attended the reading. He, along with the heir Donald Sackman, was surprised to learn the scope of Morton Sackman's property holdings.

"Well, Gramps was always close-mouthed about what he owned," Donald said to Guerevich. "I knew he owned this house. And I suspected he own a bit of property, but I had no idea about the full extent of his estate."

To no one's surprise, the will revealed that Morton Sackman indeed kept a large amount of cash in his house, over a quarter of a million dollars. The money in his safe was to go to his business partner, Edelberto Gonzalez. The astonishment came when the full extent of Sackman's property was revealed.

He owned houses in several states and in Mexico. In addition to 125 acres in Scottsdale, he owned a large house in the Belmont Shores area of Long Beach, California and a two-flat on the Gold Coast of Chicago, not far from where he had been born. In Mexico, he had a large estate on Lake Chapala, a home in Guadalajara, and another in San Miguel de Allende. The value of his total holdings, and now of Donald Sackman, exceeded one hundred million dollars.

Overnight, Donald Sackman had become a wealthy man, and Edelberto Gonzalez was headed for life in jail or death row and a lethal injection. The money he should have inherited went to a trust pending the outcome of his trial, which almost everyone believed would be short.

A week after the will had been made public, Guerevich lay in bed next to Ann, reading a biography of Albert Einstein. Suddenly, he slammed the book closed.

"You read something you didn't like?" asked Ann, sitting up with her own book propped against a pillow.

"The Sackman case is still bugging me."

"Why. The case is wrapped up and tied with a bow, thanks to good police work and the blatant evidence in Gonzalez's garage. You'll probably get a commendation."

"That's just it. It was too easy. Something doesn't seem right, but I just can't get a handle on it."

He got up to go to the bathroom, and stumbled over a pair of Ann's shoes that she had left next to the bed. "Shit."

"Well, watch where you're stepping and you won't trip."

"That's not why I said shit. Did you do a DNA test on the gloves from the Sackman murder?"

"Yeah. It was Sackman's blood. You expected someone else's?"

"No. I mean the inside of the gloves."

"The inside? We normally do, but with all the other evidence, we didn't feel the extra time and expense was worth it. What are you thinking?"

"I just had an idea. When I was in the Yeshiva, we were taught the *what if* method. Sometimes it led to ridiculous conclusions. But often it led to lively discussions and interesting ideas. So I've been asking myself some *what ifs*. Like what if Gonzalez isn't our man. What if young Sackman killed his grandfather. A couple of days ago he put the Long Beach house on the market for 2.7 million dollars and yesterday I heard he contracted for a $250,000 motor home."

"Is that so strange? The guy spent twenty years as his grandfather's flunky. Now he's got the money. Maybe he wants to live a little."

"That's another *what if*. He spent years overshadowed by his grandfather. What if he just got tired of it when he saw a lot more years of the same."

"Okay, but where's the proof?"

"There might be some DNA evidence inside the gloves. What if he wore the gloves. He and Gonzalez are about the same size, so the gloves could have been his. What if he planted the evidence. We know he was at Gonzalez' house the same day the body was found."

"That's a lot of *what ifs*."

"Yeah, but like I said, this case was too easy. Finding the money, the gloves and the weapon in Gonzalez's garage. C'mon, the guy made no attempt to hide anything. He didn't seem to be that stupid. I mean, if you're gonna kill someone, you at least throw away the weapon and the gloves."

"You've got a point. I'll get on it first thing in the morning. Now come back to bed."

Guerevich crawled back into bed and put his arms around Ann. She snuggled close to him, her ear next to his mouth.

"You'll let me know as soon as you get something?" he whispered.

She pushed him away. "Oh, shut up and go to sleep."

The next afternoon, Guerevich's office phone rang.

"Guerevich here."

"Hi, Aaron. It's Ann. I sent the gloves out to *Independent*. They said they'd get on it right away, but it'll take a couple of days to turn up something, if there's anything to turn up. But this case is supposed to be closed."

"I heard from the PD's office that Gonzalez is under pressure to cop a plea"

"So? What's unusual about that?"

"It's okay if he's guilty. But he's refusing, which leads me to think maybe he's not. I'll share my thoughts with you when the evidence comes in."

Two days later, Ann walked into Guerevich's office and presented him a with large brown envelope marked INDEPENDENT: SENSITIVE.

"You were right. Fortunately, Donald Sackman gave us his DNA sample shortly after his grandfather's death. The DNA evidence we retrieved from inside the gloves shows that Donald Sackman wore them at some time. Your *what ifs* did lead somewhere. How the hell did you come up with that?"

"The biography of Albert Einstein you gave me. I was reading the part where he said that you can't force your ideas on the universe, but sometimes, if you're receptive, an idea comes to you and says, *Here I am.* When I got up and I tripped over a pair of your shoes, that's when the thought came to me. Ziemansko and Jameson said young Sackman went into the house to turn on the light in the dining area. It was night and the house was dark. He should have stumbled over the body of his grandfather in the dark. But he didn't. He had to step over or around it to get there. Only the killer would have known that a body was there."

The new DNA evidence proved sufficient for a judge to issue an order releasing Edelberto Gonzalez. She also issued a warrant for the arrest of Donald Sackman, who was arraigned on the charge of murdering his grandfather.

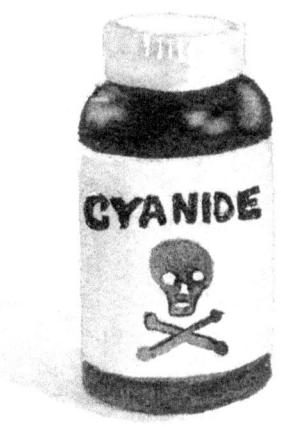

CYANIDE SUICIDE

Dominic Tintor picked up the phone, listened for a dial tone, and began dialing.

His wife, Elizabeth, shook her head. "You aren't really going to do it, are you Dom?"

"Do what? I just want to get that stupid half brother of mine out here. If he's here, I can get him to sign the quit claim."

"Do you think that's right? He's entitled to half. . ."

"He ain't entitled to nothing. He don't know nothing about it, and I want to keep it that way."

"But it doesn't seem right, Dom. What're you going to do if he refuses?"

"He won't refuse. I got a plan."

In Chicago, the phone rang three times before Frank Tintorelli, Jr. picked it up.

"Hello Frankie? It's your Uncle Dominick."

"Uncle Dom. We haven't heard from you for a while. How are you?"

"I'm okay. How's your father?"

"Papa was bummed you couldn't get here for Mom's funeral."

"Well, things were going crazy at the restaurant. I wanted to come, but I just couldn't get away. The restaurant business is like that. Anyway, how is Frank?

"He's okay. A bit depressed, but he's doing okay."

"That's one of the things I was afraid of. I remember how crazy your grandfather Anthony got when my mother died. That's why I called you instead of your father. Him and me, we need to patch things up. I'd like him to fly out here for a couple of weeks. The slow season is starting. Not too many tourists come to Phoenix for the summer, and I can take some time off. I just hired a new cook, and he seems to know his stuff. Tell you what. I'll pay for his ticket. I just had a great two months, and your dad and me, well, we need to talk face to face."

"Great idea. Thanks for the offer. I been bothered that you two seem to be on the outs."

"Me, too. So I decided, what the hell, I'll make the first move. Me and Liz, we'd love to have him here for a while. Let me know as quickly as possible."

Dominick Tintor hung up, and turned to his wife. "Maybe that will work. A free trip away from Chicago."

"I still don't think it's right."

"I'll tell you what's right. It's right that he gets nothing after the shit he put me through because I shortened my name. The way he carried on, you'da thought I stabbed his mother. Just because we had the same father? I'm the one who took care of the old man when he was dying. Frank was too busy in Chicago with that fancy wife of his and her family."

The next day Frank Junior conference-called Edward and Vincent, his two brothers. "I need your help to talk Papa into flying to Phoenix."

"Who's in Phoenix?" asked Edward, a math teacher who lived in Northbrook.

"Uncle Dominick. Actually, I think he lives in Scottsdale. I'm worried about Papa. Living alone in that brownstone in Wrigleyville. That's not good."

"Well, you're a cop. Can't you do anything? Send a patrol by or something?"

"I see him as much as I can, but it's hard with three kids and Jeanne working. I just made sergeant, and I got a lot more pressure. What about you? You don't teach eight hours a day."

"You're not the only one with a family, Frankie. I saw Papa last week, and I'm worried, too. Hey, Vince. You part of this family? Say something."

Vince groaned. "I talked to Papa yesterday. He don't sound good. But what's he gonna do in Phoenix, for crissakes?"

"What would you know, driving a beer truck up in Milwaukee."

"Don't start, Frankie. You know why I'm here. Now that I'm off probation, I got nothing in Chicago. I'm better off here."

"Papa can visit Uncle Dominick," said Frankie.

"Yeah. Things haven't been so good between them," said Edward. "That's a good idea."

"I think Uncle Dom wants to patch things up. He feels bad he didn't come to Mom's funeral. In fact," Frankie continued, "he called me yesterday to say he'd even pay for the plane fare. He and Papa were very close when they were younger."

"Yeah, it might do Papa good to get away," said Vincent.

"Like you did? You're breaking his heart by staying up there in Milwaukee."

"C'mon, Ed. I had to get away from the neighborhood, or I'd end up in the slammer for good. I got a good job here, and. . ."

"Can it, you two. I know Papa's got plenty of vacation time. It'd be good for him."

"You know money's not a problem," said Vincent.

"He won't use Mom's insurance money," said Ed. "He won't even let me invest it for him. I think he pretends it's not there. He won't let Uncle Dom buy the ticket for him. If we're going to get him to go, we ought to buy the ticket for him."

"Well, I won't be able to help much. I'm barely making ends meet as it is. Let Dominick pay for it. He offered."

"You been going to the casinos again?"

"I can handle my debts, don't you worry. I just don't have any extra right now."

Edward and Frank bought the ticket and presented it to their father. Surprisingly, Frank Senior agreed to fly to Phoenix, even though it was August, and the temperature there averaged 106 degrees.

"I haven't seen Dominick for almost three years, not since your grandfather's funeral and he shortened his name to Tintor. What the hell kind of a thing was that to do. What, he's ashamed of the family? Ashamed to be Italian? When we were kids, we were like real brothers, even though we only saw each other a few times a year."

Edward put up his hand. "Papa, don't go on about it. It was years ago. Let it go. Lots of people change their names, but it doesn't change the person."

"Maybe you're right, Eddie. Maybe it's time to fix things up. You say he called and offered to pay my way?"

"Yeah, Papa."

"Well I don't want his money."

"We knew. That's why me and Eddie got you the ticket. It's an August Christmas present."

Five days later, Frank Tintorelli Senior was dead. When his three sons were informed, they all flew to Phoenix.

Scottsdale Detective Aaron Guerevich was called in on the case, along with his fiancée, forensic pathologist, Ann Berendt who examined the scene. After the photographers finished, the ambulance took away the body.

Guerevich started questioning Dominic Tintor. "You two are related?"

"We're half brothers. Same father, different mothers. After my father and Frank's mother separated, Frank stayed in Chicago with his mother. Anthony, my father, came out here Phoenix. That's where I was born."

"What year did they get married?"

"Actually, they didn't. He never could get a divorce from his first wife. The Catholic thing."

"I see. I take it you shortened your name."

"It was easier for business at the time."

"Right. Can you tell us what happened, Mr. Tintor?"

"I really don't know. I needed to do some shopping and Frank, because of the heat, decided to stay at the house. When I came back, about three hours later, I found Frank slumped in the chair with that bottle in his hand. At first I thought he was sleeping. Then I noticed the front of his pants was all wet, and I smelled shit. Then I bent down and I smelled the bottle. That's when I called 911."

"We'll have to run some tests, but that bitter-almond smell is cyanide for sure," said Ann. "Mr. Tintor, why do you have cyanide in the house?"

"I was having trouble with field mice, and I was going to use it on bait in the traps. A couple of drops on a piece of bacon, I figured, would do the trick."

"It sure would," said Guerevich. "Where'd you buy it?"

"Actually, I got it from a friend of mine who's a photographer."

"You found him just sitting in the chair like that when you returned?"

"Yeah. Like I said, I called 911, and the ambulance got here in less than five minutes. Then the police and you showed up. I didn't touch a thing. I watch all the police shows on TV, and one thing I learned is don't touch nothing."

"And your wife?"

"She's still at work. She works Saturdays at the beauty salon. She don't know nothing about this, yet.

"Sure looks like a suicide," Guerevich said. "But did he have a reason to take his life?"

"I think he's been really depressed since his wife died of cancer last year, but you need to talk to his sons. I called them in Chicago. They'll be here tomorrow."

After leaving the building, Aaron looked at Ann. "You ready for a late lunch? I'm starved."

"A guy just killed himself and you want to have lunch?"

"Have you ever known me when I wasn't hungry?"

"Well, you seemed satisfied the other night. I swear, if I ate half of what you eat, I'd be an elephant. I can't understand how you stay so thin."

"Good genes, I guess. "Anyway, there's a new deli that opened at Fashion Square."

"You and your pastrami and hot dogs. Do you know there's a world of different cuisines out there?"

"Yeah, but that's for tomorrow. Besides, I haven't had a kosher hot dog in weeks."

When they were seated, Guerevich took a sip of his cola and shook his head. "This one beats all. The two brothers. . ."

"Half brothers."

"Right. Half-brothers. They don't see each other for three years. Then one flies all the way from Chicago to Phoenix and kills himself in his half-brother's house. Doesn't make sense."

"To me either. People who are depressed usually take their lives at home. They don't come 2,000 miles and then do it."

"Well, the cyanide was there, and maybe that gave him the opportunity. We need to talk to his kids tomorrow."

"I need to get back to the office," said Ann. "The new computer filing system is killing me."

"What about after?"

"I'll probably be stuck there until seven. What do you have in mind? I don't think I'll want any dinner."

"I wasn't thinking about dinner. Your place is right around the corner from the office, so to speak."

"There's some sliced turkey in the fridge if I'm a bit late."

The next afternoon, Guerevich and Ann met with the three sons at their hotel. Guerevich shook hands with each of them.

"I understand you're with the Chicago PD, Frank. Want to join in on this one?"

"No way. All we want to do is get Papa home."

They walked down the one flight of stairs to the hotel coffee shop and sat at a table.

Edward and Vincent agreed with Frank, confirming that their father had been depressed over the death of his wife.

"Papa's been despondent since Mom died six months ago. They been married for almost thirty years," said Frankie

"Cancer?" asked Ann.

"Cervical cancer," said Edward. "A year ago, the cancer went into remission. But it came back, and she just kind of gave up."

Edward signalled the waitress and ordered coffee for everyone. "Papa sort of withdrew after the funeral," said Edward.

"He put the $100,000 from her insurance policy into the bank and wouldn't even let me invest it for him."

"Yeah," added Vincent. "He started losing weight. He was down to 190 pounds. He used to weigh about 220."

"Like you noticed. It did seem to be getting worse," said Edward. "But not this."

The waitress brought five coffees and left after Guerevich said they were not going to order anything else.

"Yeah," said Frank. "I thought Papa was looking forward to seeing Uncle Dominick. Said he wanted to patch things up."

Guerevich sipped his coffee. "Was there a problem between your father and his brother?"

"Dominick was Papa's half-brother. Grampa Anthony married Dominick's mother after he was divorced."

Guerevich looked at his notebook. "I understood that your mother never gave your father a divorce."

Vincent slammed his cup down. "Who told you that?"

Frankie reached over and put his hand on his youngest brother's arm. "It's true. You probably didn't know it, but Grandpa Anthony never really married Uncle Dominick's mother."

Ann continued to press Frankie. "But was there a problem between them?"

"Papa got upset when Uncle Dom shortened his name to Tintor. Then when he didn't come to Mom's funeral -- well -- that really bothered him."

"Do you think he was depressed enough to commit suicide?" asked Guerevich.

"Well, he was pretty despondent," said Vincent.

Edward folded his arms and glared at Vincent. "What do you know up there in Milwaukee. You hardly ever saw him."

Frank raised his hand. "Take it easy, Ed. We're all a bit on edge, but let's not let tempers take over. I don't think that Papa would do it. Sure, he's been dejected, but not enough to kill himself."

Ann jotted in her notebook. "I'm sorry that you three have to go through this. When the coroner makes his final determination, he'll release the body to you. Do you plan to take him back to Chicago for burial?"

Frank nodded. "We've already made the arrangements."

That night Ann told Aaron some surprising news. "I did some checking on the internet when I took a break from the filing. According to public documents, when Dominick's father, Anthony, died three years ago, he owned a 300 acre parcel just outside Prescott, valued at about 7.5 million dollars. The land had been purchased in the 1930s by Dominick's grandfather, who also happened to be Frank Senior's grandfather. Dominick, who lives in Scottsdale has been the sole trustee of the estate. Apparently from what the three sons didn't say, their father never knew about the property."

"You lost me, Ann."

"Dominick put the property up for sale, but he couldn't sell it without letting Frank Senior know, and that means letting Frank Junior, Edward and Vincent know as well. Frank Senior signed a quit claim to the property a few days ago. Now that he's dead, Dominick gets the property all to himself."

"The signature is real?"

"Hard to know. The real estate company says it's real. Someone in their office notarized it."

"So Dominick had motive as well as means. Once Frank came to Scottsdale, he had the opportunity. And he played right into Dominick's hands by being depressed and despondent over his wife's death."

"But can you prove it wasn't suicide?"

"I don't know yet. All I know is something seems to be wrong, and I want to find out what. This is one I need to sleep on, Ann. You have anything that will tell us something we haven't thought of?"

"I have a text on toxicology and antidotes. I'll bring it home."

That night, as Ann slept with her face buried in a pillow, Aaron mentally reviewed his notes. Lying on his back, he stared at the ceiling, his hands behind his head. Unable to sleep, he went to the kitchen and warmed a cup of the morning's coffee in the microwave. While it heated, he booted up his laptop and set it on the kitchen table. After taking a sip of overheated coffee, he found a site on the internet that dealt with cyanide poisoning. He clicked on "effects" and read the text.

"Cyanide is a poisonous substance that is widely used in industrial processes, such as recovering ore, electroplating, and photographic development. Sodium cyanide, potassium cyanide, and calcium cyanide are found in the form of a salt that can be dissolved in water, which produces a bitter almond-like odor. A high concentration of cyanide kills almost instantly. The victim often has a look of peacefulness because all the body muscles become flaccid."

He continued reading about the mining processes and the warnings from OSHA.

"Of course," he muttered to himself. "That's why he soiled himself. His muscles all went limp." He walked back into the bedroom. "Ann, wake up."

Ann raised up on one elbow and shook her head. "What is it?"

"I just realized what was wrong. Call the Scottsdale police while I get dressed. Tell them to arrest Dominick Tintor on suspicion of murder."

"But why. What was wrong?"

"Cyanide kills instantly, right? The victims always look relaxed and peaceful."

"That's because all their muscles become flaccid."

"Right. Because if all the muscles go limp, anything in a victim's hand will fall to the floor. That is, unless it's a bottle put in the victim's hand after he's dead."

A PAGE TURNER

Saul Rabin felt his cell phone buzz. He looked at his watch and said nothing. It was 9:45 in the morning. Getting up from the table where he was having breakfast with friends at Denny's, he moved to an empty part of the restaurant before he took the phone from his pocket and spoke.

"Yeah?"

"Saul, it's Doreen. It's time. Just don't kill him, for God's sake."

"Dor, he's my uncle. What kind of creep do you think I am."

Saul flipped the case closed, said good-bye to his breakfast companions, and made the fifteen minute drive to the house of his uncle, Doctor Avram Rabinowitz, the noted Hebrew Antiquities Scholar. As Doreen had planned, the door was unlocked. His soft-soled shoes squeaked slightly on the tile floor as he walked toward the doctor's study. He reached in his large canvas carry-bag and took out a small bottle. He poured some of the contents on a rag and returned the bottle to the bag. Then he knocked twice and opened the door. To the right of the door he saw the desk with the computer, and next to the computer was the cup of coffee. Saul smiled. Everything according to plan. Near the center of the room, he could just see the top of his uncle's head above the back of the overstuffed chair. Next to the chair was a small library table which had several folio-sized books of ancient manuscripts.

"Just put the coffee on the desk, Doreen. Thanks. I'll get it when it cools a bit." Doctor Rabinowitz did not turn, his attention fixed on a large vellum-bound Hebrew book in his lap. The fingers of his left hand absently played with his large gold ring, a miniature flag of Israel in lapis and diamond chips.

Saul walked up behind his uncle, his feet now silent on the Persian carpet.

"Doreen, what's that smell?" Doctor Rabinowitz started to turn in his chair. Saul almost leaped over the top of the chair to cover his uncle's face with the ether-soaked cloth. The doctor struggled for a moment, grabbing the hands that covered his face. His ring scraped the back of the hand clamped across his mouth. But Saul was too strong for the old man. Within seconds, the doctor was unconscious. Saul dragged his uncle from the chair to the floor and set the hands of the old man's watch back an hour. Then he smashed the watch against the floor several times until the crystal cracked and the watch stopped.

In less than five minutes, Saul carefully put the priceless ancient Hebrew and Arabic manuscripts into his bag. Walking back to the living room, Saul opened the door slightly and looked outside. Silence. No one was on the street. Saul knew Tuesday morning was the shopping time for the women of this largely Jewish neighborhood on the North side of Scottsdale. He also knew this was *Rosh Chodesh*, the first day of the month of *Sivan* in the Hebrew calendar, and the men who were not working were probably in the synagogue at prayer. Saul made sure the door was still unlocked and walked to his car around the corner in the next block.

That afternoon, Detective Aaron Guerevich's phone rang.

"Guerevich here."

"Guerevich, this is Stubbs. According to your records, you went to Schechter Jewish Day School in Chicago. So you know Hebrew. That right?"

"Yes, Captain. Why are you asking?"

"There's been a robbery at the home of a Doctor Avram Rabinowitz. Some ancient Hebrew manuscripts were taken. I thought it would be better if you handled the case."

"That's a bit racist, isn't it?" Guerevich smiled.

"You know better than that." There was no humor in his voice. "And I don't give a shit what it is. If he was Black, I'd send Walters. But he's not. Now get up off your kosher ass and get over to the Scottsdale Memorial.

"On my way. I never met the doctor, but I have read some of his books. He was the one who started me reading about the dead sea scrolls and. . ."

"That's fine Guerevich. Just get over there and find out what happened."

It was late in the afternoon when Detective Guerevich spoke with Doctor Yuan Lee at the nurses' station of the Head Trauma Unit.

"Is he up to my asking him a few questions, Dr. Lee?"

"I think so, but don't overdo it." Dr. Lee pulled a chart from the wall holder and flipped open the stainless steel cover. "He's 75, and weighs 120 pounds. Fortunately, the small amount of ether he inhaled wasn't lethal, but according to the police report, he was unconscious for over an hour. He may have sustained some short-term memory impairment, so he probably won't remember the details of the incident. Don't stay more than half an hour."

Guerevich walked down the corridor to the open door of Rabinowitz' room and stood in the doorway.

"Doctor Rabinowitz? I'm Detective Aaron Guerevich."

"Detective Guerevich? I've heard of you. My colleagues in Phoenix told me about your solving the Sackman case. Terrible tragedy, a grandson killing his own grandfather."

"Yes, it is, but that's not why I'm here."

"No, I didn't think so. No doubt you need to ask me some questions. I'll tell you whatever I can, which isn't much. What a terrible thing. I can't believe anyone would do such a thing. I don't know what to do." He closed his hands into fists and beat the air in front of him as he continued. "Those manuscripts were the basis for my new book, and now my research will have to stop. All those months, and for nothing."

"Well, let's start with what happened."

"I wish I could remember. I remember sitting in my study -- actually it's an extra bedroom that I use as a study -- I have no need for an extra bedroom, so I had three walls lined with bookshelves. On the other wall I have my desk and my computer."

"You use a computer?"

"Of course. Computers have made my research so much easier. Do you know there are computer programs that can translate from one language to another?"

"Yes, I've heard. Go on about the incident."

"Of course. Well, I remember I had taken down my large Hebrew translation of Guide of the Perplexed by Moses ben Maimon - Maimonides. I was troubled by Tibbon's original translation from Arabic to Hebrew in several propositions of Book II. Maimonides gives twenty-six propositions, which are the principles on which he based his four proofs for the existence of God. You know he wrote the Guide for a student of his named Joseph, who was confused about his belief in God and how to live his life."

"Yes, doctor. I've read the Guide. But about the incident."

"You have read the Guide? That's wonderful. When did you read it?"

"When I was younger. I attended Schechter. In Chicago."

"Did you? I know it. And they had you read The Guide? So young?"

"For what it's worth, I read it again as an adult."

"So that's what made you decide to became a policeman?"

"I decided that I could honor my mitzvot better as a cop than as a student."

"So instead of the Yeshiva, you chose the Police Academy. Your parents must have been upset."

"Eventually, they accepted it as God's will. But let's get back to the incident."

"*Oy*, the incident. Breakfast I had as usual about 9 o'clock. Then I went to my study. I was in my chair, reading when I heard the door open. The door I always keep closed because of the humidity control. For the books, you understand. Doreen, she's my secretary, asked me if I wanted some coffee. It must have been about 10:30 or so. I told her I did. She always makes it so hot that I can't drink it right away. Then she left. A few minutes later, I heard my study door open again. I thought she was bringing the coffee. I told her to put it on the desk near the door and I'd get in a few minutes. Then I smelled something odd. Reminded me of a hospital. When I started to turn, someone put something over my face. That's all I remember. When I woke up, I had a terrible headache and there were police everywhere. My nephew, Saul Rabin. He's the one who found me."

"Rabin? Not Rabinowitz?"

"Not Rabinowitz. He had it shortened. Almost gave my brother a stroke. Saul's not a bad young man, but he's had a few problems. He's 27 and is still trying to find himself. I think he gambles. His poor father doesn't know what to do."

"Not much your brother can do. How many people knew you had those valuable manuscripts?"

"Everyone, I suppose. It wasn't a secret. Oy, who would do such a thing? What will they do with them? Do you think you can get them back? Such a tragedy."

"Hey, those are my questions. Anyone who would steal the manuscripts would have to know they're valuable and probably where to sell them. Do you know what was taken?"

I don't know exactly. I'll have to take an inventory when I get home and give the police a list. Several of them, I can tell you, are one of a kind. Priceless. Who would want them? They belong at Hebrew University."

"Is there anything else you can remember about what happened?"

"Not really. It all happened so fast. I remember reading, and then I remember waking up, and nothing else."

"So you think your secretary brought coffee to you about 10:30. That's very helpful. You know that your watch was broken when you fell and stopped at 9:23. The police estimated the time

48

of your attack was about an hour earlier than you think. We'll have to resolve this discrepancy."

"Well, on my time, I could very well be off. I was quite absorbed in my research."

"Of course. However, if you do recall anything else, please call me. As of now, we have notified all the major universities and museums that have antiquities departments. But these are things that may not surface for years if at all."

Guerevich left as the doctor, leaning against several pillows, put his hands to his cheeks and shook his head.

The next morning Guerevich questioned Rabinowitz' neighbors. They were of no help. The few people who were at home didn't remember hearing or seeing anything unusual. After, Guerevich made the ten minute drive to Saul Rabin's house.

Saul opened the door a few inches and looked up at the taller man.

"Mr. Rabin? "I'm Detective Aaron Guerevich." He held his wallet open so Rabin could see the badge and ID clearly.

"I've already told the police everything," he said through the opening. "Why do I need to do it all over again?"

"I just have a few questions to tie up some loose ends and fill in my notes for the report." He took out a small notebook and held it up. A moment later, Rabin opened the door and led the way to a small dining room. Guerevich stood until Rabin motioned to a chair at a wood-grained formica kitchen table.

"As I said, Mr. Rabin, I just have a couple of questions. Why were you at your uncle's house?"

"Like I told the police, I went to pick up some books for my father about 11:00 o'clock. When I found the door unlocked, I went in and saw my uncle lying on the floor, and I immediately called 911."

"What books were you supposed to get?"

"I don't remember exactly. I do have the list my father gave me."

"He wrote them down?"

"No, he told me the titles and I wrote them down. I gave the list to the police."

"But you don't remember them."

49

"One was *Herod* by Peter Richardson, I think. I really don't remember the others." Rabin reached up with his right hand to brush hair back from his forehead.

"That's a nasty scratch on the back of your hand. How'd you get it?"

"Playing with my dog."

"I don't see your dog."

"He's at the groomers. I needed to get his claws trimmed."

"Just a single scratch? I would think that you'd have three or four." Guerevich stood up. "Well, that's all I have. I may need to ask you more questions later on."

"I'm usually home most mornings. That's the best time to find me here."

After Guerevich left Saul Rabin, he drove to the home of Doreen Gray, Doctor Rabinowitz' secretary. A sandy-haired, young-looking 30-year-old opened the door. He wondered if she got carded at bars. When she invited him in and offered him a cup of coffee, he accepted and sat facing her across her kitchen table, the coffee steaming in front of him.

"Miss Gray, can you tell me again exactly what happened on the morning of the attack?"

"Well, this must be the tenth time I've told the story." She twisted a strand of hair in her fingers. "I know Avram -- uh, Doctor Rabinowitz -- likes coffee while he does research in his study, and I brought him a cup. He told me to put it on the desk. He complains I always make it too hot." She looked at the table. "It had to be about 9:30, because I was just about to leave to go shopping." She stood up, scraping her chair against the linoleum floor. "Would you like sugar or milk with your coffee?"

"They're already on the table."

She smoothed her dress and sat down. "Oh, yes, they are."

"Where do you normally shop?"

Her eyes bounced from the doorway to the window and back. "That morning I think I was going to Karshs's Bakery. Yes, I was. They always bake fresh braided egg bread, *challah*, on Tuesdays. I wanted to get some *mandel* bread. They're almond biscottis."

"Yes, I know *challah* and *mandel* bread."

"Sorry. Of course you do. The doctor loves *mandel* bread with his coffee." She looked at her hands, folded on the table, and stopped talking.

"Go on."

"What? Oh, yes. As I said, I went in with the coffee. He thanked me and told me to put it on the desk by the door. Which I did."

"Do you remember any other thing, no matter how trivial it may seem. What the Doctor was wearing, how he looked, what you were feeling. Anything.

Her voice rose a little. "No. Nothing. Well, there is one thing. It's so little I hadn't mentioned it before. I'm surprised the robbers didn't take the doctor's ring. It's very valuable."

"His ring? I didn't see a ring when I visited him in the hospital."

"It's a large gold ring with the flag of Israel in lapis and diamond chips. Really out of character for him. It was a gift from David Ben Gurion when the doctor studied at the Weitzman Institute in Israel. I remember it because the reflection from the ring caught the light from the window and made a pattern on the wall when he turned a page."

"I see. The ring was on his left hand?"

"No, on his right hand. He always wore it on his right hand."

"Then you went to the bakery."

"Yes."

After he left Doreen Gray's house, Guerevich returned to the Hospital.

"Doctor Rabinowitz, do you know where your ring is? I'd like to have it tested."

"Tested? Whatever for?"

"You may have scratched your assailant. If you did, there will be DNA evidence that we can match."

"The ring is in the hospital safe. Take it if you think it'll help."

That evening, Guerevich called Ann Berendt, a forensic scientist who had studied in Edinborough and London. They had been working together and dating for three years, ever since he returned to Scottsdale after seven years with the Chicago Police. Ann was 39, two years younger than Guerevich.

"Okay, Aaron, what is it?"

"How'd you know it was me?"

"First, only you and telemarketers call me at dinner time. I was just about to have a bowl of cereal. Second, have you ever heard of caller ID?"

"Just thought you'd like to go out for dinner. Guess I called just in time. There's a new Mexican place I've been wanting to try, but I don't want to go there alone. I've heard the fish tacos there are good."

"You asking me out for dinner?"

"I guess so. Pick you up in half an hour. Oh, do you have any notes on the Rabinowitz case yet? I have a few ideas I'd like to bounce off you."

"I thought this was going to be just the two of us."

The phone clicked. Guerevich took a quick shower, put on a clean pair of jeans and a short sleeve shirt. Although Ann lived just five miles away, the rush-hour drive took almost twenty minutes. By seven o'clock, they were seated at a bar, drinking margaritas and waiting for their table.

"How long do you think this place will last?" Ann asked.

"If it's as good as Martinez says, they'll be here for a long time."

"Martinez? He'll eat anything that's cooked if it's Mexican. And I'm not sure about the cooked part. Now, what's your problem with Doctor Rabinowitz?"

"There's something odd about the nephew finding him. First, the story he gave the police was that he stopped by to pick up some books for his father. However, his father doesn't remember sending him, so no one knows why he was really there. Besides, Saul and his uncle don't get along all that well.

"Well, Rabinowitz is a book scholar, and he's got a large number of books."

"Yeah, but he didn't know Saul was coming. You'd think his brother might have called and at least told him which books. That way, he could've had the books ready."

"What's second?"

"Second, the business with Rabinowitz' watch."

"It stopped and broke when he fell."

"Yeah, but he fell forward. Or was pushed after he was etherized. For the watch to break, he'd have to smack his wrist on the floor very hard. His arms were outstretched and the watch crystal was down, but the hair patterns on his arm showed he usually wore the watch the other way."

"You've got theories, but not enough to do anything with."

"There's something else, something that's just not right. I'm not sure what it is, but you'll know when I find out."

"Where are you going with this?"

"I don't know. I feel sorry for the kid's father. Families like his put huge importance on tradition. Believe me, I know."

"Hey, I think they just mangled your name," said Ann. "Gerbish. Like one of those little furry robots."

They picked up their drinks and followed a young Hispanic woman to a table.

After they ordered, Aaron continued their conversation. "I might be able to get something from Doreen Gray. She's Rabinowitz' secretary. I need to question her again. She was really nervous the last time."

"You going to bring her in?"

"Nope. I think it's easier to question people at their homes. They feel more comfortable, and that's when they're more talkative. She knows more than she's letting on."

"You want me to see what I can dig up on Rabin?"

"You're a sweetheart."

"You've told me that before."

Halfway through the meal, Aaron looked at Ann and smiled.

"What's that for?"

"After dinner I have a special dessert planned. It involves whipped cream."

"Non-dairy I bet. Your place or mine?"

"Yours, of course. It's closer to the restaurant."

Later, as they lay in bed, Ann looked at Aaron and started to laugh.

"What's so funny?" he asked.

"You have whipped cream in your ear."

For the next two days Ann compiled about ten pages on Rabin. Then, she called Aaron and told him to meet her for lunch at Sweet Tomato on Dunlap.

"What've you got?" he asked as he entered the restaurant and approached her table near the window.

"Hold on. Catch your breath and let's order."

After the waiter left, she started speaking. "First, let me tell you we don't have the DNA from the ring yet. It might be another week. The lab's swamped and this is low priority. Also, we need a sample from Rabin or this is a waste of time. How you going to do that?"

"Don't know. What else?"

She flipped to the second page on her clipboard. "Saul Rabin has a minor police record. He was arrested a few times for illegal gambling."

"Illegal gambling?"

"He was part of that North Phoenix Vietnamese bust. He got off with probation and community service. Two years ago he was arrested for selling stolen lap-top computers."

"What happened?"

"That was more serious. His father paid the dealer for the ten computers, and the dealer dropped the complaint. Once the civil complaint had been dropped, the police didn't pursue the case."

"Anything else?" he asked.

"I had Trang Yi do some discreet checking. His street sources informed him Rabin's in debt from gambling. About $100,000. His family doesn't have that kind of money. Even if they had, they probably wouldn't give it to him."

"So he tries to get the money by selling stolen manuscripts?"

"The people he owes are the group of so-called Vietnamese businessmen. They've been buying up store-fronts along Northern near 34th Avenue and leasing them to immigrants along with vandalism insurance. They insure collection by threatening to make crutches a permanent addition to their wardrobe."

"So now we know Rabin had motive as well as opportunity."

"Well, there's a problem," said Ann. "If Rabinowitz was drugged at 9:23 as his watch indicates, the kid has an alibi. He

54

was with two friends having breakfast at Denny's. He was seen by at least twenty people. He didn't leave the restaurant until about 10:00."

"Yeah," responded Guerevich. "But what if Rabinowitz was hit at 10:30 and his watch set back an hour. The old man had no idea how long he'd been unconscious. It could have been only fifteen or twenty minutes, more than enough time to get away with some manuscripts."

"What you need is a witness who can place Rabinowitz reading in his study at 10:15 or so, as he seems to think. And some DNA from Rabin."

"I don't think I'll be able to get either one.

At 4:00 in the afternoon Detective Guerevich went home, slipped his shoes off and lay in bed fully dressed staring at the ceiling. The only one who knew the doctor's routine was Doreen. Somehow, she and Saul were in this together.

That evening, he drove to Doreen's house. The lights were on and he recognized Saul's red Chrysler Le Baron convertible parked three houses away. He knocked on the door, and Doreen opened it.

"Hi, Miss Gray. May I come in? I need to ask you a few more questions."

She hesitated for a minute, and then opened the door. As he entered, he heard the back door close. A few minutes later, he heard a car drive away.

This time he didn't sit down, but stood looking down at the shorter woman. "Doreen, I know that you and Saul are in this together. Do you know how much trouble you're in?"

She folded her arms across her chest. "I don't know what you're talking about, Detective."

"Let me tell you just how serious this is. I'm going to arrest you. First, I need to tell you your Miranda Rights." Aaron started to repeat the litany of rights.

As he spoke, Doreen walked to the kitchen and sat down with Guerevich following her.

After he asked if she understood her rights, he continued, standing across from her. "You saw the scratch on the back of Saul's hand. The doctor did that with his ring it in their struggle.

You know the DNA from the ring will match Saul's. Because of the doctor's age and the method used, the DA will probably charge both of you with attempted murder as well as the felony. Under Arizona law, you're just as guilty as he is. You and Saul could be going to jail for a long time. Of course, if he hasn't sold the manuscripts, and they're returned, I'm sure the DA will take that into account. Your involvement was minimal."

"Do I need a lawyer?" Her voice quivered and came from trembling lips.

"Saul will be going away for a long time. For this type of felony, he'll probably do fifteen to twenty-five years in Florence."

"Florence?"

"Saul's not tough. You know what happens to people like him in prison? He'll be almost sixty when he gets out."

"Stop." Tears began to trickle down Doreen's face. She sat down and put her face in her hands. Then she began to sob. "I told him," she mumbled through her hands. Then she looked up, her face wet. "That damned gambling of his. I told him he had to stop. Now I see what it's got him."

"Tell me what happened."

"It was his idea. The manuscripts are insured. He told me no one would get hurt. He...he had to do something. These people he owes money to - they, they're animals. They came to my house and threatened us both. He offered to give them the manuscripts, but they wanted cash. He promised me that once he sold the manuscripts and paid them, he'd stop gambling."

After Saul Rabin was arrested and the manuscripts recovered, Aaron went to Ann's apartment for dinner. As they were eating, she asked, "How were you so sure that Doreen was involved?"

"It was what she said about the doctor's ring. I knew she was lying."

"How?"

"Doreen said she saw Doctor Rabinowitz turning pages with the hand on which he wore his ring. His right hand. But he was reading Hebrew, so he would normally turn pages with his left hand. Remember? Hebrew reads from right to left, and Hebrew books open from right to left. That was the missing piece. When I called the bakery, that clinched it.   That Tuesday was *Rosh Chodesh*, and they didn't even open until noon."

A PENGUIN CLASSIC

The body of Evan Seitz lay in his bed. Next to the bed, tearfully looking at their father, stood his son, William, and his daughter, Sheila. A nurse and two paramedics stood behind them. The old man's emaciated form, covered by a blanket up to his chest, made him look like a man sleeping peacefully, arms at his sides, bony wrists protruding from navy blue pajamas. His eyes, which now saw nothing in this world, were fixed on a scene no one understood. His stark white, hairless head almost buried in the middle of his pillow, his facial features smoothly relaxed. A single night stand, an old dresser, and the bed were the only furniture.

A faint odor of antiseptic filled the room, mixed with with the stale, bad breath smell of death.

Detective Aaron Guerevich, notebook in hand, questioned Yolanda Rodriguez, the nurse. "That's the way you found him? You didn't touch anything?"

"I come in at ten o'clock, like I always do. To see if he need to be changed. When I see him cold like that, I ran outta the room.

I call 911 and then I call William. I didn't touch nothing. Is okay I leave now?"

"Was anyone else in the house?"

"Only a man from museum. He bring a gift for Señor Seitz. To add to his collection in the garage. Big *pingüino. Rellenado.*"

"That's a penguin," said one of the paramedics. "It was stuffed."

Guerevich agreed she could leave. The two paramedics mumbled their condolences and left the room with her. Only Guerevich, William, and Sheila remained.

Guerevich looked questioningly at William Seitz, dressed in a plaid cotton shirt, jeans, and moccasin style loafers without socks. Slightly thinner and shorter than the Detective he looked more like a college student than a thirty-five year old lawyer.

"No. Nothing. We touched nothing, Detective." William folded and unfolded his arms as if he didn't know what to do with them. His eyes, moist with tears, never left the elderly man in the bed. "I'm a prosecutor with the District Attorney's office, and I know better than to touch anything. That's exactly the way he was when we arrived."

"And the pills?"

"The bottles of pills are just as you see them," said Sheila. "One on the bed. Empty. The other on the night stand. I had just filled the prescription for the empty bottle two days ago."

"What kind of pills were they?" Guerevich picked up the empty container in his gloved hand.

Sheila shook her head. "He was taking Thalidomide and OxyContin. The bottle of Thalidomide is still on the table."

"Thalidomide? Isn't that what caused all those birth defects in the 60s?"

William rubbed his eyes. "That's what we said to Doctor Foster. They helped Dad for a while. He started taking them last year. Doctor Foster said they might make the chemotherapy work more effectively and help the chemo kill tumor cells that had spread to his lungs. Dad actually regained some weight, and his cancer went into remission. But about four months ago, it returned. Deadlier than ever. That's when he started taking OxyContin."

"The other pills?"

"For pain. It's common for terminal cancer patients in chronic pain. When he took them, the pain subsided, but left him lethargic. He'd fall asleep in the middle of a conversation. Actually, we've sort of expected something like this."

"You expected him to commit suicide? How do you know it wasn't something else? An accident."

William walked to the window and looked out. "Unlikely. His mind was still intact. Actually, I'm surprised he had the strength to reach the pills." He paused and walked back to the bed. "Why don't we go into the living room. I really don't want to have this conversation in this room."

The two men walked from the bedroom to the other end of the large house. They sat in overstuffed fabric chairs before a cold fireplace surrounded by a few stuffed Arctic animals - a wolf, several white hares, a puffin, and a small white fox. Guerevich looked around at the wealth of pictures on the stark white walls showing a young Evan Seitz in the company of various dark-skinned men, all wearing sealskin parkas trimmed in wolf fur.

When William was seated, his sister, Sheila Workman, went into the kitchen and returned with a carafe of coffee and two cups. There was a small table, but the two men balanced the cups on their laps.

William took a sip and replaced the cup on the saucer. "Don't get me wrong. I love my father. I may sound unemotional, but actually, I'm relieved. What my sister and I hated, what Dad hated, was this disease that was destroying his body."

Guerevich put his cup on the table and jotted in his notebook.

"Yes," added Sheila. She stood next to William's' chair. "He knew he was dying, and he detested what the pills did to him. He had no choice because of the excruciating pain. Until he became sick, he was an energetic man, full of life, well respected in his field."

"His field?"

"The Arctic."

William took another sip, put down his cup, and looked at Guerevich. "As a young man, he'd been an Arctic explorer. He continued his trips to the Arctic well into his sixties, even lived there for a time, until the difficulties of the journey became too much for him."

"He lived with the Eskimos?"

"That's a term he never used. The two groups of Indians he studied were the Inuit, who live mostly in northern Alaska, Canada and Greenland and the Yupik of western Alaska and the Russian Far East. That's how he ended up as the curator of the Arctic section of the Hart museum. He actually learned to speak Inuktitut."

"I see. Well, there's nothing more I need from you two. You have my sympathy. Unfortunately, because this may be a suicide, the Medical Examiner will have to determine the actual cause of death. That means you'll both have to wait for his report to make final arrangements."

"We understand." William leaned forward and spoke in a stage whisper. "There's one thing, however, that makes this unusual. Dad gifted this house and its contents to us last year with the stipulation that after his death, his Arctic artifacts be donated to the museum and his collection of Arctic animals be auctioned."

"Auctioned? These animals?"

"These and the collection that fills the entire garage," continued Sheila. "The proceeds from the auction are to be sent to the Arctic Studies Center in Barrow. They work to preserve the indigenous cultures before they get lost to the incursion of Western society."

Guerevich looked around at the sparse furnishings in the small house. The entire house was painfully simple. A sofa and two chairs in the living room. A wooden floor with a single carpet in front of the fireplace. An old wood table and four high back chairs in the kitchen. "So all you're left with is the house?"

"It may be small, but it's worth quite a lot. My sister and I grew up here. It's enough. As far as material things, we have just about everything we want or need. When I was sixteen, I accompanied my father on one of his expeditions, and I saw how the Inuit lived. Little material wealth, but they seemed content. At the time, I hated it, but I did learn how to live with a minimum of material comforts."

"Father always chided you on being too materialistic, Billy."
She turned to Guerevich. "He's probably the only non-materialistic lawyer in the DA's office."

"Maybe," William responded. "But there's something else. The Inuit and Yupic are great carvers. I suppose on the long winter nights, there was little else to do. Dad had a collection of very old carvings, some of which may be over 5,000 years old. They were given to him by tribal elders."

"Carvings? Why did you say he *had* a collection?"

"This is something you might not have known about, Sheila. He told me recently he thought they were probably worth millions to collectors. He kept them in the floor safe, under that carpet. He hoped to give them to the Smithsonian. When I looked in the safe, it was empty."

"When did you look in the safe, Billy?"

"Right after the paramedics said Dad was dead."

"You're not as non-materialistic as I thought."

"I guess not." He looked embarrassed. "Those carvings meant a lot to Dad. And they mean a lot to us, and not just because of their value. I wanted to remove them before anyone else learned of Dad's death. Before someone else got to them. Which seems to be exactly what happened."

"Could he have hidden them somewhere else?"

"That wouldn't be like him," said Sheila. "He was a very cautious man. Besides, for the last two months, he was almost completely bedridden."

"I'll have some officers search the house. We'll let you know if we find anything. Who else had the combination to the safe?" Guerevich wrote more in his notebook.

"Besides my sister and me, it's hard to say. It just might have been left unlocked. It was unlocked when I opened it. There have been so many people taking care of him or visiting him in the last couple of months. The doctors, hospice nurses, caretakers. Even some of his colleagues from the museum. They were always bringing him gifts to cheer him up. My father might have given any one of them the combination to the safe."

"Why would he do that?"

"It's hard to say what he might have thought when he was doped up with OxyContin. He might have thought he was talking to my mother, who died fifteen years ago."

A man in a white jacket marked M.E. entered the room and walked up to Guerevich. "We're ready, Aaron. Need any more time?"

"No, I'm done. This is Sheila Workman, Mr. Seitz's daughter, and William, his son. They want to make final arrangements when you're through."

The M.E. looked at William and shook his hand. Then he looked at Sheila. "Sorry about your father. I read one of his books on the Inuit culture. Fascinating man."

"He was that," said Sheila. "But to us, he was always Dad."

Everyone left. Guerevich returned to his office at the police station to start the paperwork that always accompanied an unexplained death. He hoped the M.E. would rule this one a suicide, which would make his work much easier. He made a note to call the M.E. the next day.

Later that evening over dinner at Ann Berendt's apartment, Guerevich discussed the Evan Seitz case with his fiancée and forensic researcher.

She scooped up two helpings of spaghetti and ladled sauce over them. Then she set the two plates on the table and sat down. "Sounds to me like he wanted to end his agony, Aaron."

"To say nothing about the pain he was putting his son and daughter through," she continued. "Can't say I blame him. Do you?"

"No, I don't. I'm sure it was suicide." He twirled his fork to wrap strands of spaghetti around it. Before he put the food in his mouth he looked at Ann. "What I'm concerned about are the missing carvings. His son told me one of them was a whale bone polar bear. Almost two feet long. The others were smaller. Walrus tusk ivory. Things you could just walk off with."

"You think the son or daughter took them?"

"Then why did they tell me about them?"

"The son told you. The daughter didn't. They must have been taken by someone who knew their value."

"She was surprised when he told me. I think it had to be someone else."

"Maybe. It still could mean the daughter? Who else?"

After dinner, Guerevich cleared the table, rinsed the dishes and stacked them in the dishwasher. Then he joined Ann on the sofa, where she was watching the news on TV. He picked up the remote and pushed the mute button.

"What about one of the old man's colleagues from the museum? William told me his father might have given one of them the combination to the safe when he was doped up."

Ann put her feet up on the sofa and rested her head against Guerevich's shoulder. "I'll bet the carvings are still in the house somewhere."

"That sounds logical. With so many people in the house every day, it was risky to walk out with them. He could just wait till he was in the clear. But we searched the entire house."

"Your guys are thorough. It's possible they missed something."

"I'm going back there tomorrow. I want you to come with me and see what you can find."

"Be happy to, "said Ann. "But right now I'm going to bed. You staying or going home?"

"Who could resist such a suggestive invitation?"

The next morning, Ann called the Medical Examiner and learned that Evan Seitz had enough OxyContin in his blood to kill him several times over.

She and Guerevich visited Evan Seitz's house, looking at every possible place a two foot polar bear and other smaller carvings could be hidden. They rolled back the carpet and looked in the empty safe. They tapped on walls and looked for evidence of new plaster. Ann walked into the kitchen to examine the cupboards. Guerevich remained in the living room. As he removed a book from the bookcase, a man entered, a little taller than Guerevich but slightly round-shouldered, carrying a clipboard.

"You must be Detective Guerevich," he said. "I'm Dr. Fredrick Weber. I'm here to catalogue artifacts for the museum, although why Ramsey didn't send a clerk I'll never know.

"Ramsey?" asked Guerevich.

"Doctor Peter Ramsey. The head of the Board of Directors for the museum." He paused and looked over his glasses at Guerevich. "I thought your work was done. I do hope you won't get in my way."

"Not at all, Doctor. We're just finishing up a few loose ends on Dr. Seitz."

"Let me correct you, Detective." Dr. Weber straightened his shoulders, adjusted his glasses, and looked down at Guerevich. "It's Mr. Seitz. Just Mr. Seitz. Sad, really. The man never did manage to finish his doctorate." The condescension in his voice was clear. "Too busy traipsing off to the Arctic to help the poor indigenous natives."

"I see. Thanks for telling me." Guerevich took out his notebook.

"Now, if you will excuse me. I really must finish and get back to the museum. Although why the museum would want this stuff is beyond me."

"You're not with the Arctic section?"

"Dear me, no. My specialty is rare manuscripts. The history of cultures that could read and write."

"I just have one question. Do you know the combination to Mr. Seitz's safe?"

"His safe? Why on earth would I want anything in that man's floor safe. Probably some old Eskimo bones. Nothing of real value, if you know what I mean."

"Is that other man also from the museum?" Guerevich indicated a man who was writing in a three ring notebook.

"I believe that's Robert Henley from the auction house. Obviously, he's making a list of those damned stuffed animals Seitz was so proud of. They are to be auctioned next week."

"I can understand someone wanting the smaller animals. The puffin or the fox," Guerevich said to Dr. Weber. "But those large ones in the garage are something else. Who'd have room for a caribou or a polar bear?"

Hearing the conversation, Henly walked toward the men. "Oh, they'll probably be bought by some sporting goods store."

"Or some bar," intoned Dr. Weber.

"How are you today, Dr. Weber? Any more animals to contribute to the auction?"

"No. Nothing." Dr. Weber looked at his clipboard. "I really must get back to my cataloguing." Dr. Weber hurried into the next room.

Ann entered the room and walked directly to Guerevich. She spoke quietly. "You need to come with me to the garage."

He followed her to the kitchen, and through the door to the garage.

"Did you find something?"

"There's a very interesting specimen." He looked at where she was pointing.

"It looks like a penguin, but it's so big. What is it?"

"Oh, it's a penguin, all right," said Ann. "An Emperor penguin. You can tell by its size. Now we can go."

"But we haven't found the carvings. I don't think they're here."

"Let's go, Aaron," insisted Ann. "I'll tell you something about that penguin when we get back to the car."

When they were back in the car, Ann said, "I know where the carvings are hidden. Tomorrow at the auction, we'll know you who hid them."

"Ann, you know I love you. But how did you come up with that?"

"Simple, my dear Aaron. Apparently, you have forgotten your geography. Seitz was an Arctic explorer, right?"

"Right. And a collector of stuffed animals, among other things. So?"

"You only find Emperor penguins in the Antarctic. Now, do you think Seitz would have one stuffed Emperor penguin with his collection of Arctic animals?"

"Probably not."

"I examined that penguin, and found out just what he's stuffed with. We'll need something the size of the large carving that weighs about twenty or thirty pounds."

"I think I know where you're going with this."

"That ugly brass table lamp of yours. The one you keep in the bedroom on your night stand. I've always hated it."

"That was a Bar Mitzvah present from my Aunt Minnie."

"I don't think she'll notice. When's the last time you saw her?"

"It's been a few years. She hardly ever leaves the Senior Center in Sun City. I've never really liked the lamp, either."

That evening, Guerevich and Ann entered the garage carrying the base of the old brass table lamp. They cut the stitching in the back and removed the polar bear and several other carvings, neatly wrapped in burlap. They placed the lamp in the opening and sewed it back the way it had been.

The next day at the auction, both Guerevich and Ann were anxious to see who would bid on a stuffed Emperor penguin.

When they walked into the house, the auction was already in session. As Guerevich stood next to Ann listening to the auctioneer, Sheila Workman and William Seitz came up to them.

"I can't thank you enough for returning Father's carvings, Detective," said Sheila, her voice a low whisper. "Wherever did you find them?"

"I can't take credit for this one. Ann is the one who discovered their hiding place."

"Bone carvings make poor stuffing," said Ann. "And never underestimate the lack of knowledge of educated people."

"I don't understand," said William.

"There are some in the academic community who think they are smarter than everyone else," said Guerevich.

"You must be talking about Dr. Weber. That arrogant bastard never let my father forget that he had never earned a doctorate degree."

"Is he the one who took the carvings?" asked Sheila. "Why don't you arrest him?"

"He never took the carvings out of the house. We can't prove he removed them from the safe. But I think he outsmarted himself. Wait a minute. The penguin is coming up for bid."

"Penguin?" asked Sheila. My father didn't have a penguin."

"We know," said Ann. "Weber brought it in. I'll explain later."

After several bids from interested individuals, Dr. Frederick Weber pushed the bidding higher and higher, until he owned the penguin.

As Weber left the house, Guerevich caught up with him. "I didn't think a penguin would be worth so much, Doctor," said Guerevich. "Especially to someone whose specialty is rare manuscripts."

"Oh, this one has special value for me."

"As in Penguin Classics? I thought Emperor penguins were creatures that inhabited Antarctica?"

"Really. Now that you mention it, I think they are. I'm surprised you knew that, Detective."

"I wonder why Dr. Seitz had one, since his area of expertise was the Arctic."

The expression on Dr. Weber's face froze in an insincere smile as he opened the trunk of his car and gently placed the penguin in a waiting box, exactly the size and shape to receive it.

"Mr. Seitz, Detective. Remember? Just Mr. Seitz." He paused. "One wonders why Mr. Seitz collected most of his things. But I really must be going, Detective. I have work to do at the museum."

"Of course. Well, Doctor Weber. It was interesting meeting you. Enjoy your penguin."

A KILLING IN COINS

The train speeding from Los Angeles to San Francisco lurched, causing Mrs. Felicity Wilson, a portly fifty-year-old woman, to bump against a compartment door. It opened slightly. "Oh, my God!" she screamed. "Someone get the conductor. Something terrible has happened in Compartment 35!"

Andrew MacTarney, a slightly built man dressed in jeans and a tan sport shirt, jumped from his seat next to the compartment. "What's wrong?"

"Just look." She pointed to the partially open door.

Through the space between the door and the wall, MacTarney could see a hand and part of an arm on the floor.

The conductor, a heavy man in his late 40s, his unbuttoned uniform jacket flapping as he approached, used his clipboard to push past MacTarney. "What's wrong?"

After Mrs Wilson pointed again, he put his shoulder against the door and pushed, but the door, wouldn't budge.

MacTarney gave the conductor a tight-lipped look. "The body's blocking the door."

In moments, several people crowded the narrow aisle. Unhooking a small radio from his belt, the conductor held the red button releasing a slight squawk of static. "We have a medical emergency here in car..." He looked up to the number over the door. "Car 117. Compartment 35. Is there a doctor on the train?" The radio squawked again. "Let me check. Yes. There's a doctor. He boarded in LA -- Doctor Michael Strauss -- traveling in car 125. Two forward from 117. Have someone get him. Don't leave until he gets there." The radio squawked and then went silent.

The conductor looked through the open door again at the hand and arm. When he turned around, he bumped into MacTarney, who was standing behind him. "Don't just stand there. Go get the doctor."

The thin man stepped back, scowled at the conductor, and then left on his errand, returning in a few minutes with the doctor, who carried an aluminum case.

"I was afraid to force the door, Doctor," said the conductor. "I might hurt that poor man more than he is already."

The doctor kneeled on the floor and reached through the open doorway to touch the man's wrist. "Well, I'm afraid there's little to be concerned about," said the doctor, standing up. "I can't find a pulse. If he's dead, we probably ought to alert the authorities in San Francisco."

"Of course," said the conductor. "I'll go forward and notify our radioman."

"There's a cop from Phoenix in the next car," said one of the onlookers. "Said he's going to some kind of convention. I talked with him this morning at breakfast. I think we ought to tell him."

"Why not find some lawyers while you're at it," mumbled the conductor under his breath as he walked away.

A few minutes later, Detective Aaron Guerevich arrived with his fiancée, forensics scientist Ann Berendt. He introduced himself and Ann to the doctor.

Guerevich braced his hands against the door. "Do you think we should force the door open, Doctor?"

When the doctor nodded, Guerevich braced one foot on the wall across from the compartment and put his considerable strength into a push. The door slid open a few inches.

Ann leaned forward, putting her head into the room through the small opening the door afforded. "His clothes are scattered and he's lying face down on top of an open briefcase. His left shoulder's blocking the door. It looks like blood from a wound on the back of his head has pooled beneath his face. Let me see if I can squeeze through."

Guerevich pressed his back back against the door and forced it open a little more, giving Ann enough room to slip into the compartment, stepping over the man's arm. She spoke quietly, forcing Guerevich to lean toward the door to hear her. "This looks like a robbery homicide, Aaron. Get my notebook. And the camera. I want to take notes and pictures before we move him."

Guerevich retrieved her camera and notebook and handed them to her. She closed the door part way, and he could see the flashes as she snapped pictures inside the compartment. When she opened the door, he saw that Ann had rolled the man over on his back , letting him come to rest face up next to the empty briefcase. Guerevich and the doctor stepped into the room, leaving the small group outside. Ann closed the door completely to keep prying eyes outside. As soon the door clicked shut, she continued writing in her small notebook.

The doctor kneeled next to the man and rolled him over to his side to examine the head wound. "A killing in Compartment 35. You might need the services of Hercule Poirot."

"A doctor and a literary man," commented Ann. She pointed to a bruise on the dead man's cheek. "There must have been a fight of some kind. Looks like someone punched him before he died. If he was hit when he was standing, the blow could have spun him around before his assailant hit him in the back of the head."

The doctor nodded his agreement. "The way the back of his head is crushed, he was hit with something quite heavy."

The doctor stood up and Ann bent down to take a closer look at the wound. "Could have been a metal pipe or even a baton. His assailant must have taken whatever was in the briefcase. The room's been torn apart, so he must have been looking for something else as well. The only way the case could have ended up under him is if he had been alive when his attacker left. That would also explain the blood under his chest. He must have crawled over the case toward the door. That's why his shoulder came to block it."

"You can tell all that from this?" The doctor swept his arm around the room.

"I'm scheduled to lead a forensics seminar on blood spatter at the San Francisco conference. I can tell where he was standing when he was hit. Look at the bathroom door. There's blood spatter above where he stood, indicating he was facing the outside door when he was hit. His assailant must have spattered himself, as well."

The doctor looked from Guerevich to Ann. "I don't think there's anything more I can do here. Is there?"

"I don't know. We do have one thing in our favor, Doc. Like Monsieur Poirot, we know the killer can't get off the train until we reach San Francisco."

The doctor walked toward the sink. "That may be, but there's a few hundred people on the train. You can't question everyone. Can you?"

"You're right," said Guerevich. "We don't know what was in the case."

The doctor rinsed his hands. "Unfortunately, the only one who can tell us is dead."

Ann looked up from her notebook. "Dead people may not talk, Doctor, but they can often tell us a lot."

The doctor wiped his hands on a paper towel. "I ought to go back to my seat. My wife must be wondering what happened to me."

"In the city, police have to go hunting for a killer," said Guerevich. "Here, we have to get the killer to come to us."

The doctor looked perplexed. "How can you do that?"

"I'm not sure yet. But I'll think of something. For now, we need to say he slipped and hit his head. That it was an accident. I don't want to say a man's been brutally murdered in his cabin and there's a killer loose on the train. That's a good way to panic everyone."

"You're right," said the doctor. "As far as he's concerned, it really doesn't matter any more."

Ann put her notebook into her shoulder bag and flipped open the bunk bed. Using a wet paper towel, she cleaned the bloody wound and looked at the man lying peacefully on the floor. "The only one who knows why he died is the killer, and he's certainly not going to tell anyone."

Guerevich stepped out of the small room, leaving the Ann and the doctor in the room with the body. By this time, the small crowd had grown to include people from other cars. They were gathered in the narrow passageway, asking what had happened.

Guerevich raised his hand for quiet. "It appears poor Mr. . . .what's his name?"

"I checked the manifest," said the conductor, who had returned. "Name's Alfred Roseling.

Guerevich turned to address the group standing around. "It looks like Mr. Roseling slipped in his compartment and struck his head when he fell."

The conductor opened the door and peered in. "Oh, my God. What a tragedy."

"Yes. However, we really need to clear this passageway so people can get by. I'll need to get the names of everyone." The moment he spoke the words 'get the names of everyone,' most of the crowd melted away. "Can I start with you, conductor?"

"Certainly. Name's Franklin Morris. It's right here on my badge. Everyone calls me Frank. I been working as a conductor for the past twelve years. Name of the woman who. . ."

"That's fine, Frank. I'll ask her myself. By the way, were you on the train from Maricopa ?"

"No. I boarded in LA. Actually, this's the first time I been on this run. I'm heading home. I live in Concord."

"How much time do we have until we arrive?"

Morris looked at his wristwatch. "We're due to arrive in Frisco about twenty after five. Less than five hours."

The compartment door opened and the doctor and Ann exited. Guerevich closed the door and looked at the conductor.

"Can you lock the door to this compartment? We'll need to preserve the room intact."

Morris unclipped the set of keys from his belt. "One of these ought to do the trick." He tested several keys until he came to the right one. "I notified the engineer to radio ahead." He walked toward the other end of the car, glancing over his clipboard at Guerevich, the doctor, and Ann.

Once the three were alone in the narrow hall, Guerevich put his arm around the smaller man's shoulder. "Thanks, Doc. I have to apologize. In all that went on, I never got your name."

"Strauss. Michael Strauss. I'm an internist." The sadness in his eyes was painful. "I was just wondering what this poor man had that would make someone want to kill him to get it."

Ann put her hand on his arm. "That, Doctor, is something we're going to find out."

The doctor looked up at Guerevich. "I'll fill out any paperwork you need. Just let me know. I really need to go back."

"Is Frank the man who called you, Doctor Strauss?"

"Please. Call me Mike. Actually, I was summoned by that man." Strauss indicated the man sitting a few feet away across the aisle from a portly middle-aged woman. When the doctor pointed at the man, he stood and made his way to them.

"Name's Andrew MacTarney - that's M A C not M C. Frank, the conductor, he asked me to get the doctor from a couple cars ahead. Mrs. Wilson over here. She's the one who noticed the poor man's arm sticking out near the door."

Guerevich took out his notebook. "Yes, I already spoke to her. You two know each other?"

Mrs. Wilson shook her head. "No, we just met on the train. My seat's across the aisle from his. I was returning to my seat from the observation car I bumped against the door. When it opened a bit, I saw the hand. I think I screamed."

MacTarney nodded his agreement. "The conductor must have been nearby and heard the scream. Anyways, he come running over right quick."

"Thanks," said Guerevich. "We'll keep that in mind. And thank you for your help, Mrs. Wilson. I might want to talk to you both again later. Doctor, uh, Mike, would you mind joining Ann and me in the dining car? I could use a cup of coffee."

The doctor looked at his watch. "Well, just for a few minutes."

When they were seated in the dining car, Guerevich asked the waiter for coffee, while Mike and Ann opted for sodas.

"We have a very fine BLT on special today."

Guerevich looked at the young man's dark face. "Sorry, no bacon for me. Just the coffee, please."

The waiter made a short bow and walked back toward the galley. He returned in a few moments with the coffee and sodas.

The doctor popped his soda open. "Are you orthodox?"

"Not really. I was raised orthodox, and I've slipped a bit, but I don't eat pork or shellfish."

"My parents were Reform, very secular."

Impulsively, Guerevich reached across the table to shake hands with Doctor Strauss. "Let's start at the beginning, now that we're seated and we can catch our breaths. Ann and I work for the Scottsdale Police Department."

"I'm on staff at LA County Hospital. My wife and I wanted a trip to San Francisco for a vacation, and we thought the train would be relaxing. Shows how wrong I can be."

"We're headed there, too. Ann told you she's leading a seminar on blood spatter at the Presidio. And since I have time off, she invited me to join her." Guerevich smiled at Ann and took a sip of his coffee. Mike looked at Ann, as if waiting for her to speak.

Ann wiped the top of the can and opened her cola. She asked the waiter for an ice-filled glass. After she poured her soda, she spoke quietly. "He had to have been killed by someone he knew."

Doctor Strauss put a straw into his can of soda. "Why do you think that?"

"He opened the door to let the person in. Considering he had something valuable enough to get killed for, he'd only open the door for a friend."

"Or the conductor," said Guerevich.

"Well, whoever it was stood with his back to the window, and punched Roseling before hitting him in the back of the head. We know he didn't die right away. He bled where he fell and crawled toward the door before he died."

Guerevich pushed the coffee cup to the center of the table. "This tastes terrible. Doctor, any idea how long he'd been dead before Mrs. Wilson found him?"

"Couldn't have been more than a few minutes, half an hour at the most."

Ann nodded her agreement.

"His body was still warm when I first tried to take his pulse." The doctor stood. "Now, I really need to get back to my wife. She's understanding, but this is our vacation. Thanks for the soda. I'll be at my seat if you need me."

After the doctor walked away, Ann spoke to Guerevich in quiet tones. "Do you think it odd that Roseling crawled on top of his briefcase."

"Yeah. I didn't want to say anything in front of the doctor."

"I checked the case. Part of the lining had been pulled away from the lid and pushed back in place."

As she spoke, a tall man dressed in a western shirt and jeans walked up to Guerevich and Ann. His handlebar mustache and long light-brown hair tied in a ponytail made him look like Buffalo Bill, but without the Van Dyke beard.

"I just been down to Compartment 35. It was locked and all the conductor would tell me was you were here in the dining car. What's happened to Al?"

"And you are. . .?"

"Roger Stamms."

"Detective Aaron Guerevich, Scottsdale Police. This is Ann Berendt. She's with the forensics department."

"Police? For the police to be involved it has to be something bad. What happened?"

Stamms sat heavily on the bench seat across from them. "Police don't get involved unless it's something bad."

"I'm sorry," said Ann, who reached across the table and put her hand on Stamm's arm.

Guerevich wonder how Stamms was involved. "How long have you known Mr. Roseling?"

"Me and Al been friends almost fifty years, since we served in Korea." He wiped tears away with his fingers and slapped the table. "Shit. What happened to him?"

Guerevich leaned forward and gave Stamms a questioning look. "Your friend's dead and someone took whatever he had in his briefcase."

"Dammit. I told him and told him not to let on what he was carrying. I shoulda been with him. shared the compartment."

Guerevich pulled out a three-ring school style notebook and opened it on the table. " I'm curious why Al didn't fly."

"Al flew raids over Korea in the 50s. He had this crazy idea that he only had a fixed number of hours in the air, and that he'd used all of them up. I told him it was silly, but he refused to fly anywhere."

Ann watched Stamm's body language while Guerevich jotted notes. "We need to know what he was carrying that someone would want to steal."

"Gold coins. We was going to the regional coin show in San Francisco. He told me he had a buyer."

"Why weren't you traveling together?"

"Al didn't want us to call attention to ourselves, so we split up. He took the compartment, which he could lock, and I had a seat in the other car. That was another one of his crazy ideas."

"He must have had quite a few coins. Seems like they'd be awfully heavy," said Ann.

"Not too heavy to carry easily. See, gold coins are often valued for more than the gold content. Right now, gold is just under $1,000 an ounce. But Al had some very rare coins."

Ann took out her own notebook. "What do you mean, rare?"

"You ever hear of the Pikes Peak gold rush?"

Guerevich motioned for the waiter to take away his coffee. He ordered a soda with no ice. "I thought the gold rush was in California."

"It was. In 1849. In 1858, some Georgia prospectors discovered placer deposits of very pure gold in a ravine near Pikes Peak. The area actually came to be known as Georgia Gulch.

Problem was all the raw gold had to be transported back east to mint. That was dangerous and expensive. So one private firm, Clark, Gruber & Co. minted their own coins on site with machinery they brought from Philadelphia."

"Wasn't that illegal?" Ann wrote the names in her notes.

"Not back then. It was pretty common. There were quite a few private mints in California, like Humbert. Or Kellog. The value of a coin was in its gold weight."

"You seem to know a lot about gold coin history."

"I learned about it from Al." Stamms paused and looked at the ceiling. "Damn, what am I going to tell Al's daughter? He wanted to make sure she was taken care of. Her husband died a last year in an auto accident, and she's still waiting on the insurance settlement. She's got two kids."

Ann looked at her notebook. "Let's see if we can get the coins back for her. How did Roseling acquire the coins?"

"Al bought a cache of gold coins at an estate auction. For a long time, the most complete collection of the Clark Gruber coins has been The Frederick R. Mayer Collection. When Al went through the auction coins, he found fifteen minted by Clark, Gruber, and Company. They were in almost uncirculated condition. Those fifteen gold coins were worth about a million dollars or more. What's more, he had the provenance to go with them."

Guerevich looked up. "What's provenance?"

"That's the verifiable history of the coins. That's what proves they're genuine. Al had the coins wrapped in felt in his briefcase. But I had the provenance documents."

Ann smiled. "So that's why the room was so torn up. Someone was looking for those documents."

"Whoever took the coins knew they were valuable," said Guerevich. "But would they be able to sell them without the provenance?"

"Mister, you don't know the coin market. There's dealers and collectors who will buy things and never ask where they came from. The coins'll go into someone's collection and won't see the light of day for forty years or more."

"That's a long time," said Ann.

"Let me tell you something about coins. There's an aluminum cent that surfaced a few years ago. It was minted as a pattern in 1943. It didn't work out, and the mint presented the four or five test samples to some congressman. He gave one to a White House custodian who saved it. Today it's worth about three hundred thousand dollars. Course, most dealers is honest, but the thief could get an easy quarter million for the coins, even though they're worth four times that much."

"But they can be traced back to your friend, can't they?"

Stamms pulled a pocket watch from his jeans. "It'd be like trying to trace the ownership of my watch here. I know it was made about 1860 in Savannah, and I like to think it once belonged to Jefferson Davis, but there's no way to prove it. History books say Davis had a watch like mine. If I could prove he once owned my watch, it'd be worth fifty or sixty thousand dollars to some collector. As it is, it's worth a couple hundred as an antique."

Ann looked closely at the watch. "Were the coins insured?"

"No. Coins this valuable are impossible to insure without letting the world know what you have.

Guerevich wrote something in his notebook. "What's your involvement in this?"

"I was hoping to get something from the sale--maybe about $50,000. As it is, I'm out about $2,000, but that's no big deal. Roseling was a good friend and decent guy. Like I said, all he really wanted was to help out his daughter."

Guerevich stood up. "Well, there's nothing more we can do here. We need to talk to the conductor again. I'll let you know as soon as we find out anything."

Ann and Guerevich returned to their seats to compare notes and discuss strategy for pursuing the case, knowing they were not licensed outside of Scottsdale. Ann started to review her notes and looked at the photographs on her digital camera. Guerevich returned to Compartment 35. When he found the door unlocked, he pushed it open and looked into the room. The white sheet that had covered Roseling's body had been pulled aside to reveal his pasty white face. The briefcase was missing.

Guerevich found conductor Morris eating a sandwich upstairs in the observation car.

79

"Did you unlock the door to Roseling's room?"

Morris smiled. "Matter of fact, I did. His good friend wanted to spend some time with him, so I left him in the compartment. Figured it couldn't hurt, with him dead and all. Roger Stamms he said his name was. Said it was a shame we'll never know what he had that was so valuable."

"Really. What do you know about gold coins?"

Morris jerked his head back, his smile snapping into a stern look. He rose and started to walk away, looking at his wristwatch. "Is that what was in his case? I don't know nothing about any gold coins. I'd guess there are people who would pay quite a bit of money for them. Well, I'd better get on with my rounds We'll be in Frisco in less than two hours."

Guerevich watched him walk away and went to find Stamms. Next to him on the seat was the open briefcase.

Guerevich sat across from him and smiled. "Very convenient. Now with the coins and the documents, you make quite a pile of money."

"Wait a minute. You think I killed my best friend?"

"A million dollars is a strong motive. People have killed for much less."

"You going to arrest me?"

"I don't have the authority to do that. However, with our notes and photographs, the San Francisco police should be able make a strong case against you. And they have an excellent crime lab. Is there anyone you need notify, Mr. Stamms? Aside from Al's poor daughter, if he even has one."

"If you can't arrest me, I'm through talking to you." Stamms eyes narrowed and his face set in a hard, cold look. "I'll be happy to talk to the San Francisco police when we get there."

Guerevich met Ann and they walked back to the dining car. Sitting across the table from him, she shrugged her shoulders and called the waiter to order a cup of coffee.

Guerevich stopped the waiter. "Order something else. The coffee here is terrible."

"Oh, no sir. We make fresh. Coffee is good now."

"Okay. Two cups. And I'll have a slice of apple pie."

"No apple, sir. Peach."

Guerevich nodded. The waiter left and returned with two cups of coffee, some of which had spilled into the saucers.

Ann dabbed the spilled coffee with a napkin and then picked up her cup. She held it in front of her. "Fascinating subject, gold. I read somewhere that ninety percent of all the gold ever mined is still around."

Guerevich sipped his coffee and looked around for the waiter. "Interesting. What's really going through that brilliant but beautiful head of yours?"

Ann smiled. "This guy Stamms is a piece of work. Wouldn't you love to get him into an interrogation room? I mean, Roseling's carrying valuable gold coins in a briefcase and Stamms has the provenance. Maybe he went to Roseling's room. Roseling opens the door when Stamms announced himself."

Guerevich motioned for the waiter, who brought his peach pie. "Stamms is probably our man."

"On the other hand, why would he wait until he gets on a train where he's virtually trapped? He could have killed Roseling before they got to the train. There are certainly plenty of places to kill someone in Phoenix. Besides, he was really broken up when he found out Roseling had died."

Guerevich stabbed a piece of his pie with a fork and offered it to Ann, who declined. "You're missing out on some good pie. Who, then if not Stamms?"

"Well, we have MacTarney. And Mrs. Wilson. Don't let her age and size fool you. They all may have heard Roseling talk about the gold coins."

"I still like Stamms. He had the most to gain. In addition, he knows buyers."

"I don't agree, but let's go back to our seats and rest. You know how things come to us when we free our minds."

Returning to their seats, Guerevich leaned back and closed his eyes. The clack-clack of the wheels and the hum of electricity settled him into a state of near sleep and reminded him of train trips he took with his family when he was a teenager. He remembered watching the countryside whiz by and asking the train's speed of the conductor, an elderly Black man in an immaculate pressed uniform with a white starched collar.

With a twinkle in his eye, the aging conductor had said, "Young man, this train is moving at exactly 69.5 miles per hour."

"When will we arrive?"

"We'll arrive at 6:23 exactly."

Guerevich opened his eyes and turned to Ann. "That's it."

"What's it?"

"What was wrong. Remember, you said something was wrong? I know what it is. I need to talk to the train engineer."

A few minutes later, Guerevich returned. "Can you get a signal on your cell phone?"

"If I can't, I've paid a ton of money -- the department has paid a ton of money -- for nothing."

"Call the San Francisco PD. Tell them to put a couple of detectives on the train to arrest the conductor, Franklin Morris, on suspicion of murder. I'm betting that somewhere in his possession are the gold coins."

The train made an unscheduled stop in Oakland. Two detectives boarded the train, conferred with Guerevich and Ann for a moment, and arrested Arthur McRory - posing as Franklin Morris - as the train arrived in San Francisco The coins were discovered in the false bottom of his carry-on case. In the baggage car on a pile of old rugs, they found Franklin Morris, bound and still unconscious. McRory had drugged him, and Franklin had slept through the eight-hour train ride. Roseling and Stamms had discussed the coin show and were overheard by McRory. He claimed he only meant to rob Roseling, and that killing him was an accident.

That evening, in their hotel room, Guerevich congratulated Ann on her presentation at the blood spatter seminar.

"You were brilliant, as always," he said. "Ready for dinner?"

"Thanks, but I have a question for you that I didn't have time to ask before.

"Fire away." He opened the door and they walked down the hall to the elevator.

They stepped into the small car and Ann punched the lobby button. "Back on the train. What made you so sure that Morris -- I mean McRory -- was the killer?"

They walked through the lobby and the doorman hailed a taxi for them. Ann got in first and Guerevich walked around. He took her hand as he sat down. "When you said something was wrong, I kept turning that idea over in my mind. It took a while for me to figure it out. Remember when I asked when we would be arriving? He said twenty minutes after five. Not unusual, except railroad people never tell time that way. He should have said 5:20. He said he lived in the Bay Area, but he called the city Frisco. No one who lives there calls the city by that name. In fact, many residents are offended by the term. There was one other thing. I checked with the train engineer. McRory never notified him to radio about Roseling's death. That's when I knew he had to be the killer.

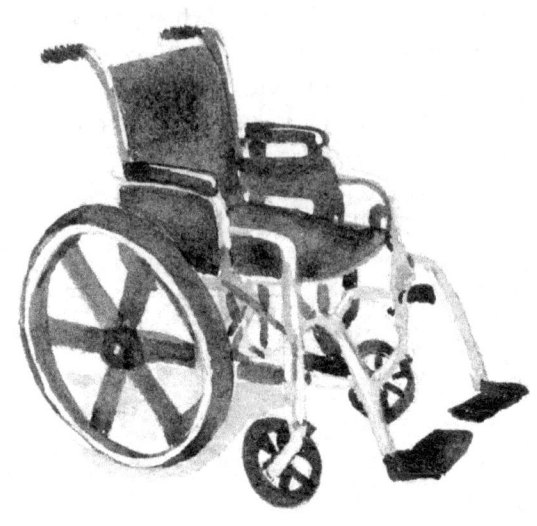

ASHES TO ASHES, DUST TO DUST

The explosion at Nick and Sonny's gas station rattled windows for an entire block in the Scottsdale neighborhood. Fortunately, no one was at either of the two gasoline pump stations when the blood-red billowing fireball erupted fifty feet into the afternoon sky.   Simultaneously, shopkeepers and homeowners scurried into the street from their buildings. Approaching sirens wailed and a police car skidded to a stop in the street.

Officer Wayne Williams surveyed the scene. "This place is history, Dan."   He looked at what once was an aluminum overhang, now twisted, one end touching the driveway. As he took a few steps toward the burning building, he kicked aside bits of splintered wood.

Dan Siebens radioed dispatch. "This is five-two-zero. We have an explosion at a service station. Mariposa and 85th. Possibly gasoline. Fire inside building. You copy?"

A female voice responded. "Affirmative five-two-zero."

Dan stood next to his partner as a fire truck and an EMT van arrived. Four firemen, dressed in protective outfits that looked like black space suits, leaped from the truck and sprinted toward the building followed by two paramedics. The firemen shouted for everyone to stay outside until they had the fire under control. After a few minutes, one fireman signaled it was safe to enter.

The officers and the EMTs slowly ventured into what was left of the building, kicking aside pieces of brick, wood, and glass. They shouted, more to discover survivors than to warn potential perpetrators.

In the back, a cinderblock wall with a doorway led to another room. The door hung by one hinge. Shattered glass shards surrounded the window in the center of the wall. The typical repair facility had a large open room with two lift racks to the left of an office. In the room, along the bottom of the wall, rested a jumbled pile of bricks, fan belts, cables, and an assortment of tools, tires and rims thrown by the force of the explosion, The metal garage doors bowed out, like a sail in a strong wind, and both lift racks were down. Fragments of the metal roof covered part of the first rack. The wall next to the further lift rack bore streaks of black, like huge fingers pointing to the missing section of the roof.

The body of a man lay pinned under the rack, his badly charred head exposed. Above him on the rack was the smoldering wreck of a car, partially covered in white foam that dripped to the floor. One firefighter walked toward them and pointed to the body under the rack. "No one's in this room except that poor guy."

As he spoke, a second fireman pushed the hanging door aside and peered in. "Someone's back here in a wheelchair," he shouted as he entered the room.

The EMTs ran into the room, reappearing moments later, one pulling and the other pushing the wheelchair. The unconscious man in it had the name NICK sewn over the left breast pocket of his work coveralls. As they rushed him outside the building and started to examine him, he opened his eyes and flailed his arms.

"Who are you?" he shouted. "Leave me alone. Oh, no. Sonny."

One EMT shouted back. "You got a bad bump on your head. You probably have a concussion. We need to get you to the hospital."

"I don't need to go to hospital." He looked toward the sky and wailed. "Sonny." He emitted the name a second time, the sound softer, between a wail and a groan. "Sonny."

After cutting a section of Nick's pants one EMT squeezed his thigh to hold the muscle firmly. He felt the muscle tense momentarily. Then the second EMT produced a syringe and injected a muscle relaxant. Nick pushed the hand away. When the first EMT started to wheel Nick toward the van, Siebens and Williams stopped them. He bent toward Nick's face. "Who else was in the building?"

"Just my brother. Sonny. Working under a car on the rack."

Siebens looked at Nick and shook his head. "I'm sorry."

A moment after Siebens spoke, Nick closed his eyes. Tears streaked down the plaster dust on his cheeks and he wiped them away with his hands, giving his face a clown-like appearance.

"Lucky you were in the back from the looks of things," said Williams. "That cinder block wall probably saved your life."

The second EMT lowered the ramp on the van, and the first EMT continued pushing the wheelchair toward it.

Nick started shouting and flailing his arms again. Then he reached down and pushed the brakes. "No hospital, no hospital."

After arguing with Nick for a few minutes, the EMTs told their dispatcher that Nick refused treatment and transportation to the hospital. They informed the police and they drove away, responding to another call.

Officer Dan Siebens looked at the man in the wheelchair, folded his arms across his chest and shook his head as he surveyed the wreckage of Nick and Sonny's two-pump gas station.

He turned to his partner. "Wayne, go see if you can get any statements from the crowd standing around gawking."

As he spoke, the two firemen returned to the truck and grabbed large prying tools to extricate the burned body from under the rack. A few minutes later, tires crunched to a stop on the dirt outside.

Siebens turned around. "Hey, Aaron, what the hell're you doing here?"

"Chief Escobedo told me to get my ass over here, so here I am. Get any statements from the concerned citizens?"

"Williams is doing that now."

"Who's that?" He pointed to a bagged body being wheeled out on a collapsible gurney.

"Not sure yet. Probably Sonny, the brother of Nick, that guy in the wheelchair."

Williams returned, notebook in hand. "Near as anyone can tell, there was an explosion that literally blew the roof off. Then the fireball. The station is owned by two Indian brothers. Nick and Sonny. It's an independent."

Guerevich looked toward Nick in the wheelchair, sitting alone crying. "They don't sound like Indian names."

"Yeah. One guy knew their real names. Nitin and Sunil Achmed. Had an attitude. Said he knew there was going to be trouble and he stayed away from the station because they were Muslims."

"Staying away is one thing," said Siebens. "Blowing up a place is another."

Guerevich looked back at the building. "What happened to the other brother?"

Siebens looked up from his notes. "The explosion likely blew out the hydraulics and the car came down on top of him. The fire roasted him pretty bad, but the EMTs said he was probably dead before the fire got him."

"Wasn't the safety bar set?" asked Guerevich.

"Don't know yet."

Guerevich hated situations like this. But more, he hated that he was sent because he was Jewish. "The department has a whole section for hate crimes," he muttered to Siebens, "but they send me."

"Maybe they think you're more sensitive."

In his wheelchair, Nick sat staring emptily back at the ruined building. Before entering the building to look around, Guerevich needed to question him. The people staring at the scene reminded him of vultures feeding on the misfortune of others. He walked toward Nick, a big-chested man in a tight one-piece blue work uniform. The sleeves barely came to his wrists. His uniform was covered in small fragments of splintered wood and white plaster dust, as if he had been baking bread. It clung to his hair, flecks covered his cheeks behind his glasses, and lay in patches on his shoulders and on his lap. As Guerevich approached, Nick brushed his clothes, white dust falling in small clouds down his pant legs to the creases in his large work shoes. It fell to the ground around his wheelchair and swirled into abstract patterns in the oily surface surrounding him.

Guerevich estimated that standing, Nick would have been over six feet tall. He reached to help him brush the white dust from his shoulders. "I'm Detective Aaron Guerevich."

"I can dust myself off very well, thank you." Nick pushed Guerevich's hand away and spoke with a strong British-Indian accent. "They took my brother away in a body bag. To die like this isn't right." He pounded the arms of his wheelchair repeatedly as he spoke. "After all he has been through. The wars and the hatred."

"What wars? And what hatred?"

"The Pakistani-Indian wars. Hatred there and hatred here. People here are hypocrites. Before nine eleven, they were happy that our gas and our labor was cheaper than everyone else's. After, for a long time, many stayed away. We got hate mail and spray paint on our windows. Things were starting to get a little better. People understood we are Hindu, not Muslim. And now this." He put his head down and covered his face with his hands, his elbows on the armrests of the wheelchair.

"I'm sorry that your brother died in such a horrible manner. It must anger you."

"I am saddened to be alone. He is temporarily with Shiva and Vishnu now."

"Any idea how this could have happened?"

"He had just completed a conversion from gasoline to propane. He must have been checking the line. There must have been a leak. Maybe he dropped a tool and it sparked on the concrete. Or maybe something else."

"Wasn't he using brass tools?"

"All our brass tools were stolen last month. We turned in a report, but we didn't expect he police to do anything. We ordered new ones."

"Well, the coroner will have do an autopsy, but the cause of death seems pretty clear.

"I want to go home. I must make some phone calls to people and tell them what's happened. I also have to make arrangements for Sunil's cremation."

"You really ought to go to the hospital. Just for evaluation, to make sure there's no serious problem."

"I am not going to hospital. I am quite well. I've had enough of hospitals in my life, and I don't need to go for a little bump on the head. After a childhood in Pakistan, death doesn't mean too much. Fear of death is a western idea. I've been in a chair since I was ten, before we came to America. My brother and I believed we were living on borrowed time anyway. He just had a shorter payment plan."

Nitin took leather gloves from a pouch hanging behind the wheelchair but decided against putting them on. Wheeling himself away from the building, one wheel struck a piece of wood that turned his chair slightly. Guerevich walked over, kicked away the stick, and Nitin rolled toward his car, giving Guerevich a look of surprise.

"Thank you, but I really do not want your help. I managed by myself before you guys came along, and I shall manage long after you're gone."

He removed one arm of his wheelchair and set in the carry bag on the back of his chair. The chair rolled backward a few inches until he reached down to set the hand brakes. He braced himself with one hand on the second arm of the wheelchair and his other hand on the seat of his car. Using only his arms, he pushed himself into his car. Then he reached out of the car door, removed the other chair arm, folded up the wheelchair, and slid it behind his seat. After the chair was in place, he picked up his legs and slid them into the car. Then he moved the seat back and drove away.

Guerevich watched, a smile of admiration brushing his lips.

Siebens walked up. "Not as upset as you might think for someone whose brother was killed and his business destroyed."

Guerevich nodded. "He didn't even ask to see the body."

"You think he was squeamish? His brother was burned pretty bad."

"I don't think it was squeamishness," said Williams, who approached and heard the conversation. "I think he was trying to distance himself. He may be in denial."

Guerevich started walking toward the building with Williams and Siebens following. "You may be right. It could be some Hindu cultural thing."

"We need to have forensics follow up on who wanted the conversion done on the car. Seems odd to do a propane retro-fit after all their special tools were stolen. Williams, I'd like you to go to the house of that 'I-told-you-so' guy. See if you can get any more information from him, and ask him to come down to the station as a person of interest. No. Tell him we need his help. Appeal to his patriotic side."

Looking at the car lift, Guerevich observed the safety bar had been removed. He wrote down the license of the burned hulk. In the back office, behind the wall that saved Nick, Guerevich went through a small metal file and found the paperwork for the car conversion. The invoice bore the name George Abbott.

That afternoon, Guerevich visited the forensics lab. Ann had just returned from viewing the crushed and burned body. "That was pretty gruesome, and I thought I was used to gruesome."

"Yeah. Do some research for me. Find out whatever you can about the Achmed brothers. When they bought the station, how they were doing financially. They had to have enemies, especially if some people thought they were Muslims."

"Sounds like you don't think it was just an accident."

"I don't think it was, and I intend to find out. There are too many odd coincidences. Like why'd Sonny -- uh, Sunil -- decided to retro-fit a car with propane without brass tools? Why was the safety bar on the lift removed? Doesn't seem logical. By the way, here's the invoice on the conversion. See what you can find out about George Abbott."

He left the lab before Ann could protest. That evening, Guerevich went to his own apartment and spent time reviewing his notes about the case. He and Ann kept their own places, believing that gave them a sense of independence.

He called her before he went to bed, asking her to meet him for breakfast. Then he stripped to his shorts, washed up, and stepped on the scale. He weighed himself twice a day, once in the evening and once in the morning, knowing his morning weight would be a few pounds lighter than his evening weight. He believed it was important to keep his weight under two hundred twenty pounds. "Two hundred twenty-three. No carbs tomorrow."

The next morning, as he sat drinking coffee, Ann walked into the restaurant and dropped a folder on the table.

"This is it? One thin folder?"

"You think I work only for you? There'll be more when the coroner completes the autopsy report."

"I think I'll go down to the morgue. Maybe I can speed things up a bit."

"More likely it'll slow things down. You have a tendency to impede progress when you don't know what you're doing. But I know you'll do whatever you want. Let me know how you make out. I've got three other cases I'm working on, so I certainly won't stand in your way."

After checking in at his office and attending a mandatory community resource meeting which he viewed as a waste of his valuable time, Guerevich went to the basement to coroner Robert Block's office. As he walked in, his nose was assaulted by the overpowering small of formaldehyde. Tears automatically formed in his eyes.

"Aaron," said Block. "Let me see if I can guess why you're here. The Achmed autopsy, right? I was planning to complete it after I finish lunch."

Guerevich wiped his eyes and nose with a tissue. "Any way you could finish it now? I'd like to watch."

"Always in a hurry. The answer is no. I'm waiting for some tissue sample results which should be back around one. I'll let you watch after lunch as long as you don't get in my way. I've got an extra sandwich, and I was planning to eat in the lab."

"In the lab? I don't think so. You really eat in here?"

Block laughed. "Just kidding, but you get used to the smell after a while. Really, I was going out to lunch. If you're still kosher, there's a vegetarian restaurant not far from here. I can tell you what I found so far."

When they were seated, a tall dark-haired waitress appeared.

"Hi, Doc. What'll it be today?"

"I'll have the grilled portobello mushroom sandwich today, Selena. You want one, Aaron? They're good. And bring some of your Guatemalan coffee."

"Just coffee for me, thanks."

When she left, he looked at Guerevich and laughed. "I don't usually discuss autopsy results over lunch."

"I won't mind."

"Well, it was hard to do a typical autopsy. We usually start the "Y" cut just at the shoulders and proceed to the groin, but he was burned so badly that. . ."

"Hold it," said Guerevich. "I'm interested in the results, not the process."

"So you don't want to know how we opened his head?"

"Not really. Maybe I should just read your report."

"You're such a wimp when it comes to autopsies. You surprise me, being a cop. You came to get information, and I intend to tell you what I found. However, since I'm such a nice guy, I'll let you finish your coffee first."

Guerevich put his cup down, and Block started. "Ready to hear about the autopsy as far as I've gone?"

Guerevich looked at the ceiling and took a breath. He folded his arms with his elbows on the table. "Go ahead."

"It was what we expected. He died as a result of massive trauma to the chest. The fall of the auto rack with a car on it crushed him pretty badly. The fire came after he was dead."

"So it was an accident?" Guerevich pushed his cup away.

Block sipped his coffee and held his cup in his hand. He spoke unemotionally. "Looks that way to me. There two odd things, though. We discovered a brain tumor the size of a small lime in the parietal lobe. That's near the back and top of the head."

Guerevich sat up. "You telling me he had cancer?"

"Probably. Those are the specimen tissues I sent to a cancer lab to find out the grade."

"Cancer is graded?"

The waitress came by with a pot of coffee. Guerevich shook his head.

Block pointed to his cup. "It indicates the degree of malignancy. If the tumor was high grade he would have been dead in a year. Maybe less. He had to know. The skull can't expand to make room for even a small growing mass. The pressure can damage or destroy brain tissue. He must have had symptoms."

"What kind of symptoms?"

"In plain terms? He might have had trouble naming things, or focusing his eyes, or hand and eye coordination, things like that."

"You said there were two things."

"Yeah. Blood analysis showed traces of Valium. Not enough to kill him." Block looked at his watch, drained his coffee cup and put it down. "Sorry to cut this short, but I need to get back to the lab. Still want to watch?"

"No, that's all the information I need."

"I'll send you a copy of the complete report in a few days." He pushed back his chair and stood, smiling. "Since you insisted on this meeting, the lunch is on your department. He walked away.

After paying, Guerevich returned to his office. A sergeant stopped him as he walked toward his office. "We brought Edward Castle in for questioning in the Achmed case. He's the one Williams identified in his report. Captain Escobedo wants you to talk to him."

Guerevich walked into the small interrogation room, which housed a six foot table and four hard metal folding chairs. A single frosted glass window, covered with wire screening, let in hazy light, and a fluorescent ceiling fixture allowed the only other light in the dim room.

Guerevich walked around the table, took a seat, folded his hands and looked at the man who faced the window.

"You want some coffee, Mr. Castle? I just had lunch in a Chinese restaurant," he lied, hoping to elicit Castle's potential bigotry. "The coffee was so weak I thought it was tea."

"Damn foreigners fuck up everything. Can't even get the goddam coffee right. Sure, I'll have a cup."

Guerevich walked over and tapped on the door. A uniformed woman opened it and in a minute, brought two styrofoam cups into the room.

"Thanks, Emily." Guerevich turned back to Edward. "This coffee will curl your hair." He set the cups down and walked around the table. Then he sat and took a sip. "So you don't particularly like foreigners."

"I don't care one way or the other. But them fucking rag heads? Calling themselves Nick and Sonny. What a joke. Y'know, my great-grandparents came to this country, and the first thing they did was learn English and try to fit in. They wanted to become Americans."

Guerevich thought he could bait Castle into betraying his bias. "Yeah. Today, people want to bring their country with them."

"You got that right. They want to be here, but keep everything the way it was where they came from. Why'd they come here is what I'd like to know. They want their own neighborhood, their own stores, their own restaurants, their own schools. They even want us to print everything in their own language."

"You're right. We need to make English the national language." Guerevich leaned back in his chair. "What about the Achmed brothers? I heard people were boycotting their station I also heard you protested in front of their gas station a few months ago."

"So what if I did? It's a free country, and I got a constitutional right to protest if I want to. I got nothing against them Pakees, but I started going to the Chevron station over on 85th. Costs a few cents more, but it's run by Americans. I felt sorry for the brother in the wheelchair, but he was probably getting free medical care that my taxes was paying for."

"What kind of work do you do?"

"Right now, I don't have a permanent job."

"How long have you been unemployed?"

94

Castle folded his arms, his mouth downturned in a sneer. "I'm not. I been working at a temp agency for the last year until I can find something permanent. I used to work at Acme Fireworks in Pahrump, Nevada."

Guerevich leaned back and sipped his coffee. "Why'd you leave?"

"Didn't like Nevada. Too much temptation with gambling."

"A couple of weeks ago, Achmed's station was broken into and their brass tools were stolen. You know anything about that? You know they did propane conversions?"

"I seen their sign. Sure. Everyone did. Look, I don't know nothing about their tools or that explosion." He paused and leaned toward Guerevich. "I'm not under arrest, am I?"

Guerevich flashed his best sincere smile. "Of course not."

"Then thanks for the coffee, but I gotta go. I got work tonight. Taking inventory at an auto parts store."

"Where were you when the explosion occurred?"

"I was home, reading the want ads, and having breakfast."

"Alone?"

"Yeah. Alone. Most people who ain't married live alone." He stood up, walked to the door, and put his hand on the doorknob. Then he turned to face Guerevich, who had remained seated. "Y'know, these people come here, take jobs away from us with their cheap labor, and then expect us to welcome them. Well, it don't work that way. Where the hell did they get the money to buy a gas station in the first place is what I'd like to know."

After he left, Guerevich spoke to Escobedo. "Any chance we can get a search warrant for Edward Castle's house. I think he's more involved than he wants to admit."

Two hours later, three latex-gloved, plainclothes policemen appeared with Guerevich at Edward Castle's apartment with a warrant for anti-Muslim material. Over his protests, they began to go through everything. In his desk, they discovered bulletins from an organization called AFA, an acronym of America for Americans. The president of the organization was listed as Edward Castle. Under his bed they retrieved a poster-sized sign nailed to a stick with the words 'BUY AMERICAN' crudely hand-painted.   In the trunk of his car they discovered a large canvas work-bag filled with tools, among which were two brass hammers and an assortment of brass screwdrivers and wrenches.   Edward Castle was arrested and charged with a hate crime involving a homicide.

Back at the station, Guerevich reviewed his notes to prepare a statement for the District Attorney. He spread the photos over his desk and stood, poring over them.   As he examined the photographs with a large magnifying glass, he looked at Nitin in his wheelchair.

Something clicked, like a seat belt snapping shut in his brain.   "Well, shit.   No wonder he didn't want to go to the hospital," he said aloud. "Look at that."

There was no one else in the office at the time to see him point to Nitin's shoes in the photo.   He sat heavily in his chair and reached for the phone to call Ann.

"Forensics," came the voice with which he had become familiar over the years.

"Hi, Ann. It's me."

"Who's 'me'? Ralph? David? I know, it's Armando."

"Very funny."

"Oh. Aaron. It's you."

He could imagine the big smile on her face.

"Just keeping things from getting too complacent," she said. "What do you need?"

"I think Nitin traded places with his brother Sunil. I think it's Sunil in the wheelchair."

"But why would he do that? It doesn't make sense."

"We need to know more about the Achmed brothers. Especially hospitals and doctors."

"Well, the autopsy did show that the dead brother had a brain tumor."

"How soon can you get on it?"

"First thing tomorrow.   We just finished the Devereaux research. There's a mixed-up set of details for you."

"Well, I think you might find the Achmed case just as confusing. I'm going up to Sedona for a couple of days. I want to do some hiking on Sunday. Being on a quiet trail helps me clear my mind. Want to come?"

"Can't. I've got two other cases to work on besides this one."

"You going to be okay?"

"Remember the line from that old song? *'Got along without you before I met you, I can get along without you now.'* At least for day or two."

The following Sunday evening, Guerevich called Ann at her apartment. "Want a little company?"

"What makes you assume I've been alone for the past two days."

"Ouch. I've given up assuming when it comes to you."

"Well, then. Come on over. I've got some casserole left, and I'd hate to see it go to waste."

Guerevich made the short drive to Ann's. Before they ate, they sat on the sofa and watched the news. Guerevich put his arm around Ann.

"I know that move," she said. "You want to know what I found out about the Achmed brothers.

"That and other things."

"Let's get this out of the way. Work first, fun later." She went into her bedroom and returned with a folder. "This one's thicker than the last one. Do you want it all?"

"It's late. Give me the short version."

"The Achmeds bought the gas station about ten years ago. Sunil was the mechanic. Nitin taught at Pima Community College. He had a degree in automotive engineering. He kept teaching and worked at the station part time. They struggled financially for a while. Sunil seemed to be the main support at the station."

"What about George Abbott?"

"There are five George Abbotts in the directory, but none of them had a propane conversion done. I ran the license plate. Sunil Achmed owned the car."

"So he was working on his own car. But why invoice it in another name? That would show income they didn't have."

Guerevich shrugged his shoulders and looked puzzled. "This gets more confusing by the minute. What about the medical?"

"That's the interesting part. We got a call from a doctor in Tempe, Ashish Shah. He saw the article in the Arizona Republic. About six months ago, Nitin went to him complaining of severe headaches. Shah scheduled him for brain scan at Scottsdale Community, but he never went."

"If he never went. . ."

"Hold on. There aren't too many places that do brain scans, I checked around. Nitin did have the scan. He went to Verde Valley MRI. I couldn't get anything from the doctor who did the scan, but his office said he might be willing to speak to you in person."

The next day, Guerevich and Ann drove to the Verde Valley Open MRI facility and met with Dr. William Mirrisch."

"All I can tell you, Detective, is that I read the MRI and the tumor looked suspicious. But without a microscopic examination, I couldn't give an exact diagnosis."

"What was your opinion?"

"It could have been anything from a grade one benign adenoma to a high-grade malignant sarcoma. But from his complaints of headaches and periodic inability to focus his eyes, my guess was a malignancy. We wanted to do a follow-up, but he never came back, nor did he ever return my calls."

"You're sure this was Nitin Achmed. Nitin Achmed, the paraplegic in the wheelchair."

"Absolutely. I told his brother that if Nitin didn't get treatment, and the tumor was malignant, he would probably be dead in less than a year."

They thanked the doctor and returned to Scottsdale. The next morning, Guerevich received the official autopsy report and opened the plain brown envelope. As he set the pictures aside, he glanced through the first page of information about the external examination. Sunil Achmed. Age 42. Height five feet three inches. Guerevich read through the medical examiner's report that the victim's legs were deformed and the muscles badly atrophied.

"That fits what I thought," said Guerevich aloud. "Nitin is listed as just a little more than five feet. But Sunil Achmed is over six feet tall. Except the names should be reversed. Sunil must have assumed he'd be able to cremate his brother's body before anyone examined it."

That afternoon, a warrant was issued for Sunil Achmed. He was brought to the station and wheeled into an interrogation room.

"You've got the wrong person," he insisted. I'm Nitin, not Sunil."

"Really?" Guerevich bent down and put his face inches from the face of the man in the wheelchair. "It's a simple thing to find out. We compare your fingerprints with those on file with the Department of Education. Nitin had to file them to get his teaching certificate. Why not just save us the trouble and tell us what happened."

Sunil slumped in the chair and hung his head, a man defeated.

"We know your brother was dying."

"Yes," he said. "He was." He looked up. Tears ran slowly down his cheeks and stained his shirt. Guerevich handed him a tissue to wipe his face. "How ironic. After all he went through. When Indian troops came into our village, he was twelve and I was only ten. A soldier came into our house and he tried to protect me. He attacked the soldier with a knife and the soldier shot him in the stomach. The bullet severed his spine. That's how he ended up as a paraplegic."

"Why'd you want to change places with him? Why'd you want to become Nitin in a wheelchair instead of being Sunil?"

Sunil took a deep breath and then sighed. "You know, Detective, for a man in a wheelchair, my brother was full of life. He was happy, productive. He always said his chair gave him freedom. Me, I was the one who was bitter. What an irony that he gets the cancer."

"I agree, but why did you pretend you were him?"

"He told me to do it for the insurance. He couldn't get life insurance because of his condition. Oh, he could, but the premiums were over a thousand dollars a month. I had half a million in life insurance. Double for an accident. That's a million dollars. If I were to die, he would have gotten it all."

"So you killed him to collect the insurance?"

"Kill my brother? The one who almost died trying to save me? No, no. This was his plan. He said it was now my turn to help him. He didn't want to wait to become totally dependent on me."

"How'd you do it from the other room?"

"A remote start. He told me my part in his plan was to get out of the way and push the button. When the engine fired, the spark caused the explosion. I didn't think the explosion would be so big. He counted on the fire to obliterate the traces of who was who.

"So was this a mercy killing or a suicide?"

"Neither. It was an accident. He said he would shout when he was ready. When I heard him yell, I started the engine."

"But he was asleep from the Valium."

"No he wasn't. He had built up a tolerance for Valium. He had been taking it for years."

"You agreed to all this? And did nothing?"

"I tried to talk him out of it. He was my older brother. How could I refuse him? This is something I'll live with for the rest of my life. Do you think I did the wrong thing? Would it have been better to watch my brother slowly become a vegetable, unable to speak, to read, to have no dignity at all in the end?"

"I can't answer that. I can tell you that you did wrong to pretend you were Sunil to collect the insurance."

"Yes. I am guilty of planning to cheat the insurance company. I never made the claim. I couldn't."

"That just means we can't charge you with insurance fraud."

"Thank you. What made you first suspect I was Sunil and not Nitin?"

"In the photograph, I saw plaster dust in the creases of your shoes. A paraplegic in a wheelchair wouldn't have creases in his shoes."

VENUS DISARMS A KILLER

Veteran detective Aaron Guerevich and rookie detective Vernon Keanes saw the uniformed guard as they stepped into the immense dining area of the 5,000 square foot house.

Keanes looked around the room.   "Jeez, look at all them statues. What'd this guy do, have his own museum?"

"Knock it off, Keanes. You're a detective now. Show some respect."

"Sorry, sir. I wasn't thinking." Keanes put his head down and stared at his shoes for a moment and then looked up smiling. "But this place? My apartment would fit in here three times over. And look at them. I never seen so many statues in a house."

Book-filled shelves lined the four walls from the floor to the ceiling, giving the room a sterile look, like a library. A few feet in front of the bookcases and lit from above, ancient statues faced the center of the room, hovering like warriors, most life size, a few larger. The center of the room held a marble-topped dining room table, surrounded by twenty-four carved-back, leather-seated chairs. A woman sat quietly at one end in a large chair with ornately carved arms.

The polished wood floor reflected the carrera statues in an eerie luminescent glow. Guerevich grimaced in working with Keanes, who had passed the detective exam barely a month before. He liked Keanes, but worried about the younger man's inexperience.

Keanes approached the guard and whispered. "Who was he?"

"Zerro Kantopolous. A collector of Greek art. I've been told most of the world was wearing loin cloths and eating raw meat when these statues were carved."

Guerevich thought about his own ancestors with a feeling of pride, forbears who had predated the Greek civilization by a thousand years. "Who discovered the body?"

"The lady at the table over there."

Guerevich turned to Keanes. "I'll talk to her. Better if I do it alone. I want you to help collect information from the crime scene. I want fingerprints, photos, everything."

Keanes face showed disappointment, but he walked through the dining room and out a door at the far end, the clicking of his shoes echoing throughout the room. Guerevich stepped around the life-size statue of Achilles kneeling over the body of slain Patroclus. At the far end of the table, almost lost in a shadow, sat the woman in her 50s, elbows on the table, head in her hands, black hair spread haphazardly in front of her. She wore a simple black cotton dress. As Guerevich approached, he noticed her black stockings and shoeless feet, her shoes next to her chair. Guerevich coughed as he approached the table. The woman looked up, pulled her hair back with her hands, and slipped on her shoes.

"Hello. I'm Detective Aaron Guerevich. They told me you found the body." He removed his worn Cubs baseball cap exposing thinning chestnut hair touched with gray, and turned a chair to sit facing her at the corner of the table. From inside his windbreaker, he took out a small notebook and a pencil.

"Yes. I am Antonia. I don't speak English so good."

"Spanish?"

"No. Greek."

"What were you doing here?"

"I come every week. Dust the statues. I don't dust all, just some each week. I keep record of ones I dust. I do them all in a month. I drop my cleaning things when I see all that blood in other room. Then I call 911."

"You didn't touch anything?"

"No. I touch nothing. Such a good man. Kind. Always he spoke Greek to me. Always offered me a coffee or a coke. Such a terrible thing. You catch who did it."

"We will." From his notebook, Guerevich tore a sheet and handed it to her with a pencil. "I'll need your name, address, and phone number."

After she printed her information, Guerevich took the page back and looked at it.

A transient smile flickered across her lips. "Arubajudaikis. Is hard unless you Greek. Just call me Antonia." She paused and looked at Guerevich, her eyes glistening. "He was such a good man. Only he have problems with his son."

"His son?" Guerevich opened his notebook to a new page.

"Nikos, his son, live with mother in Tempe. He not good boy. Always he argue with his father. Not like Jason."

"Who is Jason?"

"Mr. Kantopolous' nephew. Full name Jason Scopus Kantopolous. He is architect. Nikos, Mr. Kantopolous' son, want to play music in band. Mr. Kantopolous want him go to college, like Jason. Be teacher or doctor or something. Not play drums and make noise." She put her head in her hands and mumbled. "Such a terrible thing. Such a nice man."

"Well, Mrs. Aru. . ., uh, Antonia. You've been very helpful. Do you want someone to take you home?"

Antonia smiled. "No, thank you. For my family, it don't look so good to come home in police car. My daughter, she come get me." She left as Keanes jogged in and Guerevich pocketed his notebook.

"Chief, we found something you got to see."

Guerevich stood and looked down at the young face of his new detective, six inches shorter than his six feet three inches. He followed Keanes to a small, tiled mud room where the body still lay. Police photographer Jorge Gutierrez was busy snapping pictures of the area around the body of Zerro Kantopolous.

A knife had ripped through the back of his sweater. The tear, now covered with dried blood, lay open like a mouth calling silently for requital . Partly obscured by Zerro's shoulder, the letters *V E N* had been scrawled on the tile in blood.

"He probably meant *Venus*, Chief."

Guerevich smiled. "You think? Hell, good job."

"Thanks, Chief."

"Stop calling me chief. My name's Aaron. So, where's the statue of Venus. The naked woman without arms."

"I know that, Ch - uh - Aaron. There's a huge statue of a partially naked woman out in the center of the garden. But she's got arms and has a baby on her shoulder."

"Get one of the uniforms to dig around it. For the record, we'll just say he was stabbed and bled to death."

Thinking to show off his knowledge and have little contest with the photographer who had been born in Mexico, Guerevich asked Jesus Gutierrez how many of the statues he could name.

The young man surprised Guerevich. "I had a very good classical art education at the University of Guanajuato before I came north to become a photographer. That big one in the corner with the shield and sword looks like Mars, except he's wearing a toga. The one next to it on the pedestal, the one with the staff and curved wing-like things on his boots, is Mercury, but I've always seen him portrayed as a very young man, and this one's got a beard."

"Very good. I'm impressed. You recognize the three old women?"

"That's easy. The three fates, Clotho, Lachesis, and Atropos. One spun the thread of your life, one measured it out, and one cut it off. Looks like Kantopolous came to the end of his thread."

Keanes interrupted their conversation, hurrying in with a smile that stretched his lips. "We found the knife."

"*The* knife?" asked Guerevich. "You mean you bagged a knife? You did bag it, didn't you?.

"*A* knife," Keanes corrected himself. "Of course I bagged it. We found it buried in the dirt at the base of the statue. There's blood on it. Look here at the handle." He tightened the plastic bag so the handle could be seen easily. "The initials J. S. K."

Guerevich pulled out his notebook. "Jason Scopus Kantopolous, the old man's nephew."

"You think he's our man?" asked Keanes.

Guerevich shot him a look that could have turned him into one of the statues. "I've always found the easier it looks, the harder it is."

Two hours later after some research Guerevich and Keanes sat in the interrogation room with Jason Kantopolous.

Guerevich started the questioning. "Well, Jason, you want to tell us what happened?"

Keanes jumped in. "And explain how your knife got buried under the statue of Venus."

Before Jason could answer, Guerevich put his head out of the door and asked for a coke. He asked Jason and Keanes if they wanted anything. Both men declined.

Jason, dressed in a short sleeve shirt and jeans, sat in the metal folding chair, his hands folded neatly in his lap. He stared at the table.

"I don't know what happened." He shook his head. His neck-length black hair fell over his face and he brushed it back with his hand. "Except my uncle Zerro is dead and I can't imagine who could have done such a thing."

"Why not?" asked Guerevich. "Didn't anyone have a reason to see him dead?"

Keanes added, "You stand to come into quite a bit of money now, don't you?"

"You don't know what you're talking about. He wasn't just my uncle. When my father died in Viet Nam, he's the one who took me in and raised me."

"What about your mother?" asked Keanes.

Jason started to squirm. Guerevich made up a reason for Keanes to leave the room when he thought that he and Keanes together might be too overbearing for Jason. Although he was clearly disappointed, Keanes obliged.

When Keanes left the room, Guerevich continued. "Tell me about your mother."

"Who knows? She disappeared after my father died. Everything I have is due to Uncle Zerro. He's the one who encouraged me to go to college, to become an architect. He's the one who loaned me the money to start my own company."

"Why would he give you so much attention? A young man, barely out of college? Why not his son, Nikos?"

"My cousin Nikos could have had everything. The house, an education, money, everything. But he said he wanted music to be his life. He turned his back on the things important to his father."

"Like what?"

"Nikos refused to continue in Greek school when he finished middle school, and Aunt Sellene sided with him like she always did. Uncle Zerro believed a college education was important, maybe because he never went. Nikos said he didn't need college. When I told him he could major in music, he told me what he did was none of my business. I didn't see him very much after my aunt and uncle divorced. Nikos chose to live with his mother. Maybe that's why Uncle Zerro gave me all the help. He was the most wonderful, the kindest man I ever knew. When he set up his trust, two years ago, he named me executor."

"So that's why you stabbed him."

"You really think I killed him?" Jason put his elbows on the table and held his head in his hands. His tears added dark spots to a coffee stain on the wooden table.

Aaron stood and walked behind Jason. He put his hands on the back of Jason's chair. His shoulders stretched the material of his suit jacket when he leaned close. "You owed him a large sum of money. We found the silver steak knife buried under the statue in the garden. It had blood on the blade and your initials on the handle. And no doubt your fingerprints as well."

"I don't know how one of my knives got there. Uncle Zerro presented me with a set of dishes from Greece and the set of twenty-four knives when I graduated from college. He said I'd need them to impress clients when I entertained. And you think this was how I repaid him for all his help? Do you know he never once asked me for the $100,000 he loaned me, although I was settling with him as well as I could."

Tears welled up again in Jason's already red eyes. Guerevich walked around the table. Palms on the table, he towered over Jason, who still had his head down.

"We checked bank statements. In the past three years you gave him $5,000. At that rate it would take you 60 years to liquidate the debt. Maybe you saw a quicker way. Maybe he did ask you for the money and you got mad. Or maybe it was just an accident."

"No. No, no, no. Nothing like that. I had nothing to do with his death." He looked up. Tears ran freely down his face. He wiped his cheeks with the palms of his hands.

"The statues in his house are worth millions." Guerevich sneered, his tone contemptuous. "You sell a few to museums and you become a rich philanthropist. Your uncle's been collecting for a long time."

"The statues were a reminder of his childhood in Corfu, and of Greek history."

Guerevich softened his tone and changed the subject. He sat down, hoping to get Jason to relax. "Are you interested in Greek history?"

"Of course. I went to Greek school when I was young. But I wasn't a Greek mythophile like my uncle."

"What did you call him?"

"A Greek mythophile. Everyone called him that. Greek history and myths were his passion. If it wasn't Greek, he had nothing to do with it."

"So." Guerevich's tone became conversational. "You stabbed him and buried the knife under the statue in the garden. According to the insurance company, it was from the second century BCE and had an estimated value of about three million dollars."

Jason's red eyes widened. "I had no idea it was that valuable."

"Really. Didn't you have it appraised last year?"

Jason shook his head and spoke just above a whisper. "I think I'd like a lawyer. And I'd also like to see my wife." He shot a pleading look at Guerevich. "Please."

Moments after he asked for a lawyer, the door opened and Keanes walked in with an officer, who took Jason back to his holding cell. Guerevich stood in the hallway and watched him being led away.

"I think he's guilty," said Keanes, who had watched and listened to the interrogation.

"I have to agree. Pretty lame saying he didn't know about the knife. Although he seemed really surprised about the value of the statue."

Late that afternoon, with his wife and his lawyer at his side, Jason was arraigned on the charge of homicide. His wife arranged his bail, and they walked out of the courtroom together, her arm around his waist, his arm over her shoulder.

That evening over dinner at their favorite Mexican restaurant, Aaron dined with Ann Berendt, who was both his fiancé and a forensic researcher. He valued her insights as well as her expertise in the lab, so he always shared information about his cases. When he told her about the interrogation, she agreed with his assessment.

"Sounds to me like he's lying. Who else would benefit from the old man's death? What does the son get?"

"From what Jason told me, nothing, but I want you to check it out."

"What's to check? Jason gets out from under a hundred thousand dollar debt and becomes the executor of a multi-million dollar estate at the same time. There are people who'd kill their own mothers for a lot less."

"Yeah, you're probably right. Look how easily Keanes found that knife under the statue. Too easily if you ask me."

"Ease up on Keanes. I think he admires you. Let's order. I didn't have time for lunch. We just lost another lab person. Quit to work for Merck in their AIDS research department. I'm looking at the chimichanga."

"I'll stick with the cheese enchiladas."

"Afraid you'll accidentally eat something you shouldn't?"

"That, and I need to cut down a bit."

"What happened, you gain two pounds?"

"Let's not get into that. Who's paying for this one?"

"You are. It's your turn."

"I thought it was my turn last time." When he saw the grimace on her face, he said, "Okay, okay. Tomorrow, I also want you to get information on both the Kantopolous cousins."

Two days later, while Aaron cooked a breakfast of scrambled eggs and vegetables, Ann brought out her notebook and put it on the table as he served up the meal.

He smiled. "We didn't talk much last night. How'd you sleep?"

She punched his shoulder. "If you didn't sleep as if you were dead, you'd have heard me. I must have been up three or four times."

Guerevich shrugged and pointed to the notebook. "That the stuff on Kantopolous?"

"Much as I had time for. There are other people who need research done besides you."

"Yes, but how many of them serve you breakfast?"

"Well, there's Allen. And don't forget George. . ."

"Okay, okay. I give up. Just tell me what you found out. I don't feel like reading the whole report."

"Lazy *and* arrogant. If you weren't so good in bed, I'd dump you like old potato peelings." She brought a carafe of coffee from the kitchen, kissed him on the cheek, and sat at the table.

As they ate, she explained that from the time Jason was twelve until he turned eighteen, he had spent every summer in Greece with his grandparents. After high school, he attended Northwestern University, where he met Shirley Cantwell. They married when he was twenty-two.

"Cantwell. Doesn't sound Greek."

"You know, there are some people who aren't ethnocentric."

"Sorry. Part of my upbringing." The admonishment from his parents to marry someone Jewish jumped into his head, and he grinned at her across the table.

"Your father still nudging you about when we're going to get married?"

He nodded, pushed his plate away, and sipped his now cold coffee. "About Cantwell?"

"She majored in fashion design. He majored in architecture and also studied Greek art and history. A year ago, Jason added his wife as a secondary administrator of Zerro's trust. That means if something happens to Jason, Shirley becomes the sole trustee of the multi-million dollar estate. That's standard."

"What about Nikos?"

"He's is another story. A few scrapes with the law, but Zerro always bailed him out. Drugs and alcohol. One court mandated rehab not to mention driving school. He's twenty-seven, but he still lives at home with his mother in Tempe."

"I think it's time for me to ask him a few questions."

"There's one more thing. The letters $V E N$ that Zerro wrote in his blood showed microscopic cotton fibers. They might have come from the floor, a cleaning cloth or mop, but we're checking further. Just thought you ought to know."

The next day, Guerevich drove to an older section of Tempe. Nikos and his mother lived in a small two-bedroom pink stucco house that attempted to look Mexican but failed. One of the fake posts had fallen from the side wall and lay in the withered grass. A large rusty bolt protruded from the hole, just below the roof line. He parked in the street and walked up to the house.

The smell of stale cigarette smoke attacked Aaron as the door opened part way, held by a security chain. Guerevich could see a woman with a deeply lined face and scraggly graying black uncombed hair, wearing a worn pink terrycloth robe

"What is it?" Her voice was harsh and raspy, typical of a heavy smoker.

"Mrs. Kantopolous?"

"I haven't been Mrs. Kantopolous for over ten years. It's Patrides now. Who are you?"

"I'm Aaron Guerevich with the Scottsdale police. I'd like to speak to Nikos."

"What about? Nikki has been clean for over a year."

"It's about Zerro."

"Yeah, I heard." She slid the bolt and opened the door. "Well, come in. I'll see if Nikki's awake. He played last night and he didn't get in until almost three."

"You wait up for him?"

"Ever since Mr. Patrides was killed in an auto accident two years ago."

Sellene Patrides had dark areas under her eyes and skin prematurely wrinkled from smoking. Her still shapely body told Guerevich she had once been an attractive woman. She knocked at Nikos' bedroom door and told him who was waiting. Then she went into the kitchen to make coffee.

Nikos appeared wearing knee-torn Levi's and a stained, once-white tee shirt. Scratching his head, he walked into the living room and plopped on the sofa. "I'm not quite awake yet. I played a gig until. . ."

"Yes, I know. Your mother told me."

"So the old man's dead, huh. Well, I can't really say I'm sorry, not after the way he treated me and Mom. Too bad none of his gods came down to protect him. How'd he die?"

"Stabbed to death. I understand he paid for your rehab last year."

"He did that out of guilt. Mom told him not to, but like always, he had to do things his way. Maybe he figured if he paid for it, it'd change the way I felt."

"I take it you two didn't get along."

"Sure we did. As long as he stayed in his fucking museum and left us alone."

111

"Nikos!" His mother scolded as she walked into the room with mugs of coffee. Then she excused herself and left the room.

Nikos yawned and stretched. He sat up and leaned forward, elbows on his knees. "We didn't want his money, and we certainly didn't need his phony concern. The time for his help was long past."

"Well, Nikos, I'll make this quick so you can get back to sleep. Can you tell me where you were the night he was killed?"

"That's easy. I'm in a group called 'The NU Rockers.' That's *N - U*. We were playing a gig at the Rose Hill Tavern. The group got there about five to have dinner and set up. Started our first set about seven, and finished about midnight. By the time we packed up and left, it was around one. Then we got a bite to eat. I made it home about two or two thirty, I guess. You think I might have done it?"

"Well, it is possible, isn't it?"

"I guess, but why?" He leaned back in the sofa. "I wouldn't get anything. And if I was going to waste him, I'd have done it long ago, when I was drinking or on drugs. You ought to talk to my cousin Jason and his snooty society wife."

"We talked to Jason. I was kind of hoping he might have told you something."

"I've hardly spoken to him in years. We don't run in the same circles. He turned out to be the clone my father wanted me to be."

"Must make you kind of upset. All that money and you don't get a cent."

"Not really. Money's not my thing. Like I said, talk to Jason."

Sellene reappeared. Guerevich was impressed with the transformation. Her make-up now in place, she wore a white blouse and a dark blue pleated skirt that came to her knees, and carried a jacket to match. "I'm off to work. For your information, Detective, I do office work for a temp agency. I'm off tomorrow, Nikki, so we can spend some time together."

"Sure thing, Mom. We can get a late breakfast somewhere."

She turned to Guerevich. "I'm sorry to hear about Zerro. We had our problems, but that was all in the past. He might have been a controlling bastard, but he certainly didn't deserve to be killed." Then she walked out the door.

Nikos stood up. "If that's all, I need to get some rest. Got another gig tonight."

"So music's paying the bills?"

"Mostly. Mom works to fill in the gaps. It's getting better. We just cut a demo CD. If it takes off, who knows?" He turned and walked back toward his bedroom. "Let yourself out. The door locks automatically."

On the way back to his car, Guerevich phoned Ann. "Check on a group called 'The NU Rockers' for me? That's *N - U*."

"No hello Ann? No how's your day going, Ann?"

"Sorry. I just got through with Nikos Kantopolous. He didn't have much use for his father. I need to know if they played a gig at the Rose Hill Tavern on the night Zerro was killed. Apparently Zerro treated him and his mother pretty badly."

"That's motive, isn't it? Now we have two suspects."

"Could be. But if Nikos was at the Rose Hill Tavern, he's got an alibi. I'm going to verify the time of death with the M.E. Come by after work. I'll cook something."

"How about taking me out. It's your turn to pay again. I'm in the mood for some Thai food."

"You and Thai food. Thank goodness they make vegetarian things spicy enough to suit my taste. I'll pick you up at seven, and we can go to Malee's."

"They're usually too crowded. How about Swaddee?"

That night over fresh spring rolls, Ann told Guerevich that Jason's group did play at Rose Hill Tavern the night Zerro was killed. She removed a shoot of lemon grass from her *Tom Ka Kai* and took a sip of her soup. "Nikos didn't show up until half a hour before they went on."

"He didn't tell me that. So he could have had time to do it. The M.E. set the time of death at between three and five the day before the body was found."

That night, Guerevich stayed at Ann's apartment. While she slept, he went into the kitchen and made chamomile tea in the microwave, transferring his notes to his laptop while the water heated.

113

"Two people, both with motives and opportunity," he mumbled. He finished his tea and went back to bed.

The next afternoon, Guerevich drove to a new subdivision in Scottsdale and pulled in to a circular drive. A ceramic tile, set into the cement post at the base of the drive, bore the initials *J. S. K.* above the word *ARCHITECT*. Guerevich knocked on the door, and was greeted by a petite attractive woman in her late twenties or early thirties,, dressed in a flowing silk pantsuit. Her brunette hair had smoothly blended gold streaks, and her flawless tan skin made her look as if she had spent time in the sun. She wore owl-shaped glasses that gave her a studied bookish appearance.

Guerevich introduced himself.

"Oh, yes. You're the one who questioned my husband, Jason."

"I need to ask you a few questions." He stepped forward, forcing her to open the door to let him enter. She walked in front of him to the living room. Through large windows on the other side of the room, Guerevich could see Camelback Mountain.

"The maid is off today. I just made some coffee. Or would you prefer something else."

"A coke, if you have one."

She motioned him to a seat on the curved leather sofa. Moments later, he heard ice clink into a glass and she reappeared with two glasses filled with coke.

"Now, what did you need to ask me?" She sat on the other end of the sofa, facing him, and crossed her legs, the material from the oversized legs floating through the air.

"Your husband is in quite a bit of trouble. If he's convicted of homicide, he'll spend the rest of his life in prison."

"Surely you don't think Jason could have killed Zerro. I really don't know what I can say. I went to Sedona to visit friends a few days before the poor man was murdered. When I heard, I returned immediately."

Guerevich looked at his notes. "You and Jason are co-trustees of the estate?"

"I'm a secondary trustee. Now, I'm afraid I'll have to do all the work myself."

"What work?"

"Why, selling the statues. The San Diego Museum of Art has offered over two million for the Venus in the garden." She smiled and her voice became breathy. "The goddess of love. It's worth a lot more, but the museum would be a wonderful venue, don't you think?"

"Jason said he wanted to keep the statues in the family."

"That's what Zerro wanted. Jason never knew what he wanted. You have to understand that he only did what his uncle desired. Jason became the architect Zerro never could be. That's why he paid for Jason's college. If Jason had wanted to become a lawyer, like his father, he would have had to pay his own way. It was architect or nothing." Her voice took on a steely tone. "Zerro's philosophy was my way or the highway.'"

"I thought Jason's father was killed in Viet Nam."

"He was. He was with the Judge Advocates Service, and his offices were hit by Viet Cong mortars.

"And Zerro set Jason up in business, as well?"

"Yes, but with strings attached. Jason had to account for every penny he spent. The trust owned everything. Once a month, he had to give Zerro a written account. It was so damned demeaning. Even personal expenses and groceries had to be accounted for. My God, Jason was completely under that man's control. He didn't have the nerve to say *no*. He said it was no different from getting a grant where every cent has to be accounted for. If we needed something extra, we had to make sure Uncle Zerro approved. When we furnished this house, he examined every stick of furniture."

"But Jason had his own business. He did make money, didn't he?"

"Not enough. Jason considered the money to start the business as a loan rather than a gift. Unfortunately, the interest Zerro charged could never be paid."

"He charged interest?"

"Not the way you think. Bank interest can be repaid. Zerro charged emotional interest. Jason was like a dog happy to have a bone when the master has a steak."

"What about Nikos?"

"He despised his father. Can't say I blame him. Zerro put him and Sellene through hell because he couldn't control them."

"What will happen if Nikos challenges the trust. After all, he is Zerro's son. He should get something."

"I discussed that with Nikos. When Jason and I became trustees, I told Nikos that he and Sellene would be well taken care of if something happened to Zerro. I'm sure you know Nikos had a problem with drugs and alcohol, but I understand that he no longer uses."

Guerevich stood up. "Thank you for your time. You've been very helpful. I appreciate your talking to me."

"Of course, Detective. Anything I can do to help. I hope you don't take my comments in the wrong way. Zerro may have been controlling, but I can't imagine why anyone would want to stab the old man in the back."

Guerevich looked at Shirley and smiled as he walked to the door. As he drove south on Scottsdale Road, he called Ann to meet him for lunch at Pepe's. Over flan, he told her about his meeting with Shirley Cantwell-Kantopolous. "I don't think Jason's our man."

"He certainly had motive and opportunity. His knife. His initials. The lab report confirmed that the fingerprints on the knife were his. And it was definitely Zerro's blood. What more do you need?"

"You think his motive was money? He loved the old man and he had everything he wanted. Zerro's death didn't help him at all. Think of it as a chess game. Every move should improve your position."

"But Zerro wrote *V E N* in his own blood. He could have seen Jason bury the knife under the statue of Venus before he died."

"That's the strange part. He couldn't see the garden from where he was lying. Selling the statues'll make them multi-millionaires. Do me a favor. She said she drove to Sedona a few days before Zerro's murder. Check to see if she really was there. I think she and Jason planned it together."

The next day, Ann called Guerevich and asked him to meet her at the lab. He sat at her desk and looked at the screen saver of the two of them skiing on her computer.

"Well, Aaron, your hunch seems to be wrong. Shirley Kantopolous was visiting friends in Sedona when Zerro was killed. She got there two days before the murder, and left the day after."

"She was there the entire time?"

"The day of the murder, her friends had business in Prescott, so they left her to do some shopping in Jerome about noon. She met them at their home in Sedona for dinner."

"It takes less than four hours to drive from Jerome to Scottsdale and back. They were apart for at least six hours."

"Aaron, I think you're pushing. She would have had to drive to Scottsdale, hope that Zerro was home, kill him, and then drive back. There's no way to check the mileage on her car without knowing what it was before she left home. How could she know Zerro would be home."

"She didn't. Unless she called him."

"I think I'll be able to get a warrant from Judge Wallner to check her cell phone log. I'll let you know this afternoon."

"Great. How about if I make dinner?"

"Aaron, your cooking is limited to boiling hot dogs and frying eggs."

"What about my spaghetti. I thought you liked it.

"I was being polite. Anyway, I have a roast in the crock pot."

Ann picked up Shirley Kantopolous's cell phone and took it to the lab. She plugged it into her computer and looked at the screen as Guerevich watched.

"Looks like there weren't any calls from her cell phone to Zerro on the day of the murder. She called him three times in the previous few weeks, but nothing the week of the murder."

"Do you have that list of Zerro's incoming calls from the day of the murder?"

Ann walked to her desk, pulled out a folder, and handed it to Guerevich. He ran his finger down the listing and stopped in the middle of the page. "What's this three minute call at 1:18?"

"Looks like a call from a pay phone," Ann said. "The M.E. put his time of death at between three and five. I'll check with Phonewest. I know someone who works in auditing."

"An ex-boyfriend, no doubt."

"Well, I did have a life before you stumbled onto the scene. But this friend happens to be female."

Half an hour later, Ann had her answer. The call had come from a pay phone at Cordes Junction, a small community on I-17 about an hour north of Scottsdale.

"So she called him. I think it's time for me to question her and Jason together. I'm going to play truth or consequences and try to flip one against the other."

The next morning Shirley and Jason Kantopolous sat in the interrogation room with their lawyer Alberto Rede.

Guerevich stood outside the interrogation room when Keanes joined him. He patted Keanes on the shoulder. "You ready for this? Their lawyer is there with them. You know how this one is going to work."

They entered the room. Keanes asked if anyone wanted coffee. He and Guerevich remained standing.

Shirley glared up at him. "I thought you had asked me all the questions you needed to."

Guerevich leaned toward Albert Thinnes, the lawyer seated between Jason and Shirley. "Hello, Al. Haven't seen you for a while."

Keanes folded his arms and looked at Shirley. "Some interesting information has turned up."

"Like what?" Jason asked.

Albert held up his hand like a traffic cop stopping cars. "Neither of you have to answer any questions," He turned to Keanes and Guerevich "You both know better. Shirley's not under arrest, is she?"

Keanes smiled and leaned on the table toward Albert. "No. But we need to clear up some discrepancies with what she said earlier. Like saying she was visiting friends in Sedona when she was really alone in Jerome."

Albert glanced at his notes and looked up. His voice took on an aggressive tone. "She's already explained that. And Jerome's a long way from Scottsdale. Her friends had business in Prescott. She went shopping. That's not a crime, is it?"

Keanes looked directly at Shirley, ignoring the lawyer's comment. "And you called Zerro from a pay phone in Cordes Junction. Why call him from a pay phone instead of your cell?"

Albert stood up. "You don't even know it was Shirley. You're just guessing. I think we're through here. You have no right to question them unless you charge them with a crime."

"Do you want us to charge her with first degree murder, Al?" Guerevich turned to Shirley. "Is that what you want?"

"If you're going to charge her, do it. If you had any evidence against her, she'd have been charged already."

Keanes stood back, leaned against the wall, and refolded his arms. "We have no intention of charging her with the murder of Zerro Kantopolous. We already have someone in custody for the crime. His son, Nikos. We arrested him this morning."

Jason stood, pushing his chair back. "You can't be serious."

"Why not. He had motive. And he had opportunity. All we need to show is how he got your knife. Knowing his past problems with drugs and theft that shouldn't be too difficult."

Jason sat down heavily in the metal folding chair and put his head in his hands. "That's not right. It's just not right. He had nothing to gain by killing his father."

Guerevich jumped into the interrogation. "That's not true, is it, Mrs. Kantopolous. You told me that you and Jason planned to see to it that Sellene and Nikos would be taken care of in the event of Zerro's death. That would go a long way to developing a music career."

Albert tried to intervene, but his protestations to stop talking went unheeded.

Jason looked down at his wife. "Shirley, what's he talking about?"

Shirley kept her head down and spoke to the table. "I might have mentioned to Nikos that if anything happened, since we were trustees of the estate, we'd make sure he and Sellene wouldn't be forgotten." She looked up at Guerevich. "I know he hated his father, but I never dreamed he's do something like this."

A momentary smile crossed Guerevich's lips.

Jason's voice became pleading. "But Nikos is being charged with murder. He'll go to jail."

Shirley raised her voice, nearly shouting at Jason. "No one's going to jail. They have to prove he's guilty."

"Someone's going to jail," said Keanes. "We found the white glove with Zerro's blood and the fibers match those on the floor. We have Niko's DNA. Once we match it to the sloughed skin tissues inside the glove, we'll have all the evidence we need."

Jason shouted. "That's impossible. That wasn't his glove."

Albert's voice was firm and even. "You two have said enough. As your attorney, I'm telling you not to say another word."

"It doesn't matter now, Al," said Shirley, tears streaming down her cheeks. "What's done is done. That mean, selfish, son-of-a-bitch is dead." The icy resignation in her voice froze a sneer on her lips. "I only wanted that old man to let Jason sell a few of his precious statues. I was tired of begging for everything we needed. Jason could have at least earned a commission. That Venus in the yard was worth three million dollars. Jason's share would have paid off our debts with enough left over to have a life of our own. But Zerro wouldn't part with any of them. He said Jason'd have to wait until he died."

"And you helped him along." said Guerevich.

"No. I only wanted to meet with him. To try to convince him to do what was right for once in his selfish life."

"And you just happened to bring along one of Jason's knives?"

"No. Yes. I had it in my purse. I hoped to match the design in napkins as a birthday present for Jason."

Keanes prodded further. "But the old man was inflexible, wasn't he. Insulting as always."

"Insulting? You don't have a clue. He never liked me. I wasn't Greek. He thought I was scum, only waiting for the family money."

Keanes jabbed again. "So instead of waiting years, you shortened the wait."

"No. It wasn't like that at all. He ridiculed me. Told me he'd continue to make us squirm for every penny knowing Jason'd do nothing."

"But you did."

"I started to leave. He just stood there, his hands on his hips, smirking. And I would have left until he told me he'd let Jason off the hook if I divorced him. Said he'd give me a hundred thousand dollars cash if I asked for a divorce. Called me a whore. When I didn't answer, he turned to walk away. I was so angry and upset, I don't remember what happened after."

"But your fingerprints weren't on the knife. So you put on gloves before you took it out of your purse."

"I don't remember. I think I was wearing gloves all the time. I often wear white cotton gloves in the mountains because my hands get so cold."

"You used the gloves to write the blood clue, hoping to let Nikos or Jason take the blame."

"I was so angry, I didn't think about who would be blamed. I just wanted to get away from him."

Keanes nodded. We'd like you to write a statement attesting to the facts you just related to us. Then sign it."

As Shirley was taken away, Albert turned to Guerevich. "What you just heard was an admission that my client was under severe emotional distress." He followed her down the hall.

That evening, after dinner, as Ann rested her head on Guerevich's shoulder. "I would have sworn it was either Nikos or Jason. What made you even suspect they were not the ones?"

Something Jason said that made me think the bloody clue was phony."

"The bloody VEN?"

"Yes. Jason called his uncle a Greek mythophile. He eschewed anything that wasn't Greek, especially if it was Roman. He would have tried to write Aphrodite, not Venus."

"Of course."

"The clincher occurred when she said Zerro had been stabbed in the back. Only four people knew that. When she said that, I knew she was guilty.

www.ingramcontent.com/pod-product-compliance
Lightning Source LLC
Chambersburg PA
CBHW061253170626
46809CB00007B/2979